# Also by Ellis Blackwood

**The Samuel Pepys Mysteries**
Book 0.5: Mr Pepys's Stolen Diaries
(via ellisblackwood.com)
Book 1: The Brampton Witch Murders
Book 2: The Plague Doctor Murders
Book 3: The Coffee House Murders
Book 4: The King's Court Murders (January 2025)

Scan the QR code for social links and website.

# The Brampton Witch Murders

The Samuel Pepys Mysteries Book 1

Ellis Blackwood

Vintage Mystery Press

ISBN: 978-1-0687027-0-9

Cover design, editorial & historical fact-checking: Tim Brown, A.S.C. (Rtd).

Additional editing: Charles Johnston.

Cover illustration licensed from shutterstock.com.

For Soren, my favourite budding author.

# Contents

1. Pepys Tells of the Witch-Finder    1

2. By Coach from Cripplegate    10

3. To Brampton    22

4. Simon Hopkins    33

5. The Pepys Household    37

6. Rebecca Thacker    51

7. Goddie Grimston    57

8. Hopkins's Arrival    64

9. Incident at Supper    69

10. Aftermath    77

11. The Good Physician?    83

12. The Stablemaid    95

13. Will Farlow    102

14. Hopkins's Witch-Hunt    109

15. Pitchforks at Dawn    115

16. Magistrate & Wife    121

17. A New Curse                    131

18. Hopkins Interrogates           135

19. To Huntingdon                  140

20. Hopkins Challenged             153

21. A Door Slams Shut              162

22. Figures in Shadow              165

23. The Visitor                    171

24. A Seal Broken                  176

25. By Starlight                   182

26. A New Threat                   185

27. The Cottage                    190

28. To Battle                      193

29. A Few Ales                     201

30. The Morning After             204

31. Near Hysteria                  208

32. The Unravelling                211

33. Post Mortem                    223

34. To London                      228

Are you ready for...               230

Ellis Blackwood                    231

Acknowledgements                   233

# Chapter One

# Pepys Tells of the Witch-Finder

*L* *ondon, September 1666*

Samuel Pepys shuddered as he pulled the thin pamphlet from his library shelf, such ill-conceived malevolence did it contain. Its title was printed on the cover: *The Discovery of Witches*. And the name of its author: Matthew Hopkins.

Pepys well knew the story, having read the pamphlet many times.

Hopkins, the self-proclaimed Witch-finder General, had died in 1647, yet his name lived on. He and his accomplice, John Stearne, were responsible for hunting down at least a hundred witches, whom they had mercilessly interrogated and sent to the gallows. The true number may have been even three times higher, had records been more efficiently kept and shared.

His pursuit of these poor wretches had taken Hopkins on horseback through the counties of Suffolk, Norfolk, Essex and Cambridgeshire. And to Huntingdonshire, where Mr Pepys's parents and sister, Paulina, lived in the village of Brampton.

Only yesterday, Pepys had learned that Paulina stood accused of witchcraft, and that her very life hung in the balance.

It felt as if the ghost of Hopkins had returned to torment him.

It was the morning following the fire that had broken out on Pudding Lane.

That same night, Pepys had charged his new protégé, Jacob Standish - son of his recently deceased friend and colleague, Sir Miles Standish - with the retrieval of his precious stolen diaries and capture of the thief. It was Pepys's way of looking after the somewhat ungainly young man, while putting him to good use. It would enhance Jacob's character and provide for him a trade: that of *inquisitor*.

When Jacob proved hesitant to accept the responsibility, Pepys allowed his young housemaid, Abigail Harcourt, to join the investigation through London's night-time streets. She was unusually quick-witted, he was aware, and more familiar with the city's seamier corners.

To his delight, their mission had been a success. While Jacob discovered previously untapped observational skills, Abigail proved to be the finer inquisitor, so Pepys was happy to allow the pair to reunite for this new case: to save his sister from the hangman's noose.

Pepys rose around six o'clock on Sunday 2nd September, after learning about the fire in the city during the early hours of the morning. He had viewed the conflagration across rooftops from an upstairs window of his house on Seething Lane, and deemed it sufficiently distant not to concern his own welfare. So he had returned to bed.

Jacob joined Pepys for breakfast that morning, seated at a fine oak table in the dining room. They talked not of the fire, but of Matthew Hopkins and Paulina Pepys.

The room was dark-wood panelled, illuminated by daylight through twin leaded windows overlooking the street. As Clerk of the Acts to the Navy Board - among the navy's most senior administrators - Pepys presented a household that befitted his position. Maps and paintings of naval vessels hung on the walls and a gleaming brass quadrant (polished by Abigail) took pride of place on an ornate sideboard. Elsewhere were stacked plates, dishes and pewter-ware, in preparation for meal times.

His house, on three floors, stood within the Navy Board's estate. It boasted ornamental gardens, which Pepys would show off to visitors, sited just west of the

Tower of London. In that sprawling stone fortress both Elizabeth I and her favourite explorer, Sir Walter Raleigh, had been imprisoned, and Henry VIII's second wife, the luckless Anne Boleyn, had been executed.

Pepys, 33, wore a billowing, off-white linen shirt and silk breeches. He had not yet donned his periwig, revealing matted brown hair he had attempted to comb. With his ready grin, he had the look of a man who enjoyed life.

Jacob, eleven years his junior, was inclined to be a little more dour. He was wearing the same clothing from the night before, having slept in a guest room: faded black coat and waistcoat, with saggy breeches. He too was bare-headed for the morning meal, and his sandy-coloured hair was unkempt and greasy, as was commonplace. He was tall and robust, though occasionally his limbs seemed to take on a life of their own.

Were you charging into battle, the sight of such a man beside you, fearless and imposing, would gladden your heart. Only a while later, when you realised he had tripped and lay face down in the mire, might you reconsider. That was Jacob Standish.

As the kitchen maid, Mary Blythe, served them bread rolls with butter and leftover cold roast beef, Pepys handed Jacob his copy of *The Discovery of Witches*. Its crudely fashioned pages presented Hopkins's defence of his trade, in response to growing scepticism and outrage.

Inside, the title page read:

*In Answer to severall QUERIES, LATELY*
*Delivered to the Judges of Assize for the County of NOR-*
*FOLK.*
*And now published By Matthew Hopkins, Witch-finder,*
*FOR The Benefit of the whole KINGDOME.*

*M. DC. XLVII.*

"See what Hopkins did write beneath the year," urged Pepys.

Jacob read aloud: "'Exodus 22.18. Thou shalt not suffer a witch to live.'"

Pepys groaned. "As I informed you, Mr Standish, my sister, Paulina, has been accused of witchcraft and her prospects are grave indeed. A burden upon my patience, she may be, but I would sincerely not wish the poor woman any harm."

Jacob chuckled, causing Pepys to stare daggers. "But, sir. The country is changed since the dark days of Hopkins. Witchcraft still causes fear in people's hearts, yet they are disinclined to condemn the accused. When was the last poor wench hanged for witchcraft? Surely many a year since?"

"Indeed," Pepys agreed. "Science and reason have since taken hold, and those accused have been justly acquitted. However, I am lately informed of a new peril arising from the home of Matthew Hopkins in Manningtree, Essex: his son, Simon. The boy is grown to a man and, fuelled by the spirit of his father, has renewed the witch-hunts. Though many are against him, he pays them no heed. And he does use the same dire methods as his father."

Pepys, ironically, was describing a man possessed. That man, Simon Hopkins, had Paulina Pepys in his sights.

While Jacob was broadly aware of witchcraft, he had not researched the subject. Pepys, an avid reader and self-educator, of course had, and keenly passed on his knowledge. "You must know your enemy, Mr Standish," he told his young protégé.

Principally, Pepys had studied King James I's seminal 1597 tome, *Daemonologie*. The same book had inspired Matthew Hopkins to ply his trade, informing him of ways to identify a 'genuine' witch.

One method involved binding the accused's limbs and tossing them into a pond or river to see if they would sink. If they floated, it was believed that water - essential to Christian baptism - had rejected them, marking them as a witch. If they sank, they were cleared of the charges, but might - and in many cases, did - drown.

Although using water to prove guilt was effectively illegal, Hopkins brazenly denied ever employing the method.

He was a God-fearing Puritan and his path a righteous one. Witches, Hopkins declared, had sworn allegiance to the Devil, forsaking God and Jesus Christ. The land would be cleansed of their evil.

'Thou shalt not suffer a witch to live.'

Explaining these horrors to Jacob, the naturally ebullient Pepys worked himself into a lather. He began furiously prodding the *Discovery of Witches'* frontispiece illustration, his bulging cheeks ruddy and his dark eyes blazing. It depicted two seated women wearing simple country attire, watched over by Hopkins as they called to their animal familiars.

These familiars – or imps, which children believed lived secretively in every field and hedgerow – were agents of the Devil and a sure sign of witchcraft at play. The imps pictured on the frontispiece comprised an ungodly menagerie bound to strike fear into any man's heart. Each was named.

Among the mutations were Jarmara, a fat, shaggy dog-creature with no legs, and Vinegar Tom, an elongated greyhound-type monstrosity with the head of an ox. In The Discovery of Witches, Hopkins described Vinegar Tom later changing into a headless four-year-old child, who ran half-a-dozen times around the room and "vanished at the door".

"No sane man can believe such nonsense!" railed Pepys (though the women depicted – Elizabeth Clarke and Rebecca West of Essex – had indeed been hanged). "Hopkins and his accomplices did deny those poor wretches sleep for many days and nights, until they would confess to any such devilry as he did warrant!"

Jacob, taken aback by his mentor's fiery passion, was rendered speechless.

"Have you nothing to say, Mr Standish?" asked Pepys.

The two men became aware of a figure in the doorway. The housemaid, Abigail Harcourt, had been standing there for some time.

Aged 19 and petite, she had striking turquoise eyes. She wore a servant's outfit of petticoat, dress and stockings, all woollen against the autumnal chill, and a linen kerchief covered her tied-back red hair. She had been up since dawn, going about her duties – despite three hours of sleep – and had become intrigued by her master's ranting on the floor below.

In deference to both men, she lowered her gaze. "Good morning, Master Pepys. Mr Standish." Then she added boldly, "From what you've just said, we can't get to Brampton soon enough."

Pepys managed a thin smile, seeing something of his younger self in the girl. Abigail's father, a printer, had taught her to read and write, and she was a keen autodidact, which Pepys encouraged. Astute and confident, despite her lowly status, he secretly rather admired her.

Pepys and his wife, Elizabeth, had been childless, and he sometimes wondered whether his regard for Abigail reflected the pride he might have felt in a daughter.

"Haste is indeed of the utmost importance," he said. "Though the Brampton magistrate, Bulstrode Bennett – an indecent fool with whom I am unfortunately acquainted – called for Simon Hopkins, I heard tell that the witch-finder rides first to Cambridge. If you make haste, you may prove Paulina's innocence even before his arrival. Else... you know my fears."

"Then we should leave," urged Abigail. "My bag's packed."

Pepys clasped his hands together earnestly. "And I have sent word ahead that you are both to be treated with the same respect any Pepys would command. You are my trusted employees."

Abigail raised an eyebrow; she could only hope it would be the case. "Are you ready, Mr Standish?" she asked. "The coach from Cripplegate departs at ten of the clock."

"I will finish my breakfast first," Jacob replied haughtily.

Pepys glared at him.

"Or I could take it with me," he conceded, pocketing a lump of beef and rising.

Chapter Two

---

# By Coach from Cripplegate

D istant, urgent voices echoed as they left Seething
Lane, and a great pall of smoke rose in the west.
London was accustomed to fires, its buildings being
largely wooden. As far back as the 12th century, city
elders had decreed that dwellings should be built from
stone to prevent fires. Yet citizens ignored this and chose
the cheaper timber option.

Strong winds fanned the flames towards the city's heart
and down to the Thames, where warehouses burned, and
the intense heat ignited oils, alcohol, and tallow stored
inside. The heat grew so fierce that pigeons began falling
from the sky.

London Bridge itself was on fire. Fortuitously, a large
gap between its buildings halted the fire's spread, sparing
the south bank of the river.

While Jacob and Abigail rushed on foot towards their
appointed carriage, Samuel Pepys climbed the Tower of

London for a better view of the fire. Suitably concerned, he then hurried by water to Whitehall to warn King Charles II himself, whom he had come to know through his work for the navy.

London was burning.

Witnessing the unfolding devastation at first hand, the inquisitors agreed to travel east, following the curve of London Wall to their destination of Cripplegate. It would ensure maximum distance between themselves and the conflagration.

Jacob bemoaned having no time to return home to collect supplies for their trip. The shirt on his back, he had already worn for several days. Abigail suggested he be grateful to live so far from the travelling flames. (Standish resided in affluent Westminster, outside the city boundary.)

Having followed Hart Street, the inquisitors reached Aldgate, the city's easternmost gate. London's Wall had been built by the Romans to enclose the ancient city of Londinium. Over the centuries, it had been expanded and rebuilt. Within its walls lay bustling commerce; beyond them, green fields and grazing animals, driven down from as far as Wales and Scotland, being fattened for market.

Aldgate itself, like all of London's great gates into and out of the city, was set within the Wall. An imposing stone structure with towers on either side of an arch, it was wide enough to allow the passage of coaches and carts.

London's citizens were out in force. Market stalls sold everything from turnips to tools, and the smells of baking bread and cooking filled the air.

A hackney coach stand near the gate thronged with drivers tending their horses while awaiting their fares.

"I walked quite enough last night," said Jacob, climbing inside one. "Today we take a carriage."

Abigail, whose shilling-a-week wage meant she walked everywhere, was happy to agree. Time was running short - they had just an hour to catch the ten o'clock stagecoach to Huntingdon.

Following the curve of London Wall westwards, Abigail and Jacob passed Bishopsgate and Moorgate, two of the city's northern gates, and the towering churches of St Augustine Papey and All Hallows. From the raised ground, they could see the burning spires of churches closer to the river. They could smell the smoke and hear the distant, frantic cries of Londoners fighting the blaze or fleeing.

If the wind direction did not change, Jacob feared, it would not be long before the financial district around Lombard Street, even the popular centre of commerce, the Royal Exchange at Cheapside, were reduced to rubble. The city as he knew it was disappearing.

This was a disaster like no other.

"How much of London will remain when we return?" Jacob wondered aloud.

Abigail bit her lip. "I'm worried about Master Pepys's house. Will it survive?"

Their coachman must have overheard, as he called back. "Be one of them foreigners that started it," he said. "Frenchman. Or Dutch, most likely."

"Indeed," Jacob replied.

Abigail, accustomed to such prejudice among her fellow Londoners, said nothing.

Cripplegate was one of London's busiest gates, leading north towards the popular suburbs of Islington and Hoxton. The route eventually led to Chester, from where boats could be taken to Ireland. Its main arch featured an iron portcullis that could be raised and lowered in the event of attack.

The structure boasted numerous windows and accommodation at the top. In one such room lived the powerful man who policed the Thames: London's Water Bailiff, who was also head of the Worshipful Company of Fishmongers.

Today, Cripplegate was busier than ever, with people fleeing the city for safety. They jostled and argued while traders, seemingly blithely untroubled, continued hawking their wares.

"Is that our coach?" asked Abigail, indicating a large stagecoach just north of the gate with four large horses tethered in front. It turned out that it was.

Their wooden, enclosed coach had two large, eight-spoked wheels at the back and two smaller ones at the front. Its body was painted functional red with black wheels, resembling a larger version of a hackney coach.

There was no glass in the windows, only wooden shutters to keep out the elements. Although it looked heavy and ungainly, to Abigail - who had never ridden a stagecoach - it also looked like adventure.

Inside, there was room for six passengers.

When Abigail stepped up onto the footplate, ushered there by Jacob, she found an old couple already inside, sitting opposite one another. They were arguing.

"Why did you not bring a cushion for me, Humphrey?" the lady demanded.

Humphrey winked at Abigail. "Since your *derriere*, Millicent, is padded enough!"

At which, Millicent began assaulting her husband with a bag.

When Jacob entered the carriage, cutting an imposing figure, the old woman ceased her assault in mid-air. Returning the bag to her lap, she coughed pointedly and wrinkled her nose.

"Oh dear," she said, eyeing the dishevelled inquisitor. "How unfortunate."

The fellow travellers were Humphrey and Millicent Worthington, both in their early sixties. He was jolly and portly, with bushy grey nose-hair that resembled a tiny moustache. He sweated profusely, despite the cold air that made their breath condense, and was constantly mopping his brow. He wore a velvet waistcoat with a watch chain overtly displayed and a feathered velvet hat, which he declined to remove.

"Take off your hat, Humphrey!"

"I will not, Millicent." Again, he winked at Abigail. "It keeps my head on."

Millicent slapped his leg. "Stop winking at that poor girl! She has no interest in you!"

The long-suffering woman carried an air of faded elegance. Her silver hair was tied in a tight bun, and her delicately lined face tapered towards an upturned nose. Her cold lips were permanently pursed.

Both wore outfits of style and elegance, if some years out of date.

As the coach set off towards Stevenage, where they would lodge that night, Mr Worthington bellowed, "I must tell you about the cloth trade!"

Though both inquisitors groaned inwardly, that is precisely what he did.

Until retiring in 1656, Humphrey told them, he had been a successful cloth merchant. He had risen up the ranks to become Master of the Worshipful Company of Clothworkers, one of the Great 12 Livery Companies of London. These were the most powerful and influential trades companies in the city, holding great sway over daily life and business.

He went on to explain the art of dyeing, the intricacies of wool grading, and the subtle variations in quality between the coats of different breeds of British sheep. He covered the finishing of cloth and the art of weaving. He detailed the processes of fulling, napping, shearing and pressing.

"Pray stop, Humphrey," implored his wife. Having considered Abigail and Jacob distinctly beneath her, she was beginning to feel sorry for them.

Still he went on. The banquets, the trade deals, the charitable work... It was an exhausting whirlwind of self-congratulation and Abigail wondered whether they would ever be set free. At roughly four miles per hour, she calculated, it would be another day and a half before they reached Brampton. She dearly hoped the Worthingtons were not travelling that far.

There was no escaping it: Humphrey Worthington, Master of the Worshipful Company of Clothworkers, was king of the coach – and a right royal bore.

Just outside Stevenage, as luck would have it, he was shot by a highwayman.

The dirt road had worsened as they rode further from London, forcing the coachman to stop and repair a wheel damaged in a rut. That was when Humphrey's assailant struck, cantering towards them in a cloak and cocked hat, his face obscured by a white scarf.

These renegade horseback robbers were a constant threat on the main routes out of London, and particularly on the Great North Road that Abigail and Jacob were following. These were men fallen on hard times, often soldiers unable to find work after the last English Civil War, desperate and dangerous.

"Fill the bag!" the highwayman growled, thrusting a flintlock pistol into Mrs Worthington's face with one hand and a canvas sack into her husband's lap with the other.

"Do something, Humphrey!" she shrieked.

Jacob leapt up, forgetting the low roof, smacked his head, lost his balance, and fell backward against the door. It flew open and he fell to the ground, where he lay, befuddled.

Seizing his opportunity, Humphrey Worthington lunged for the highwayman's pistol, which discharged, firing a ball of lead harmlessly through the open door opposite. Abigail fancied she felt it disturb the air at the tip of her nose.

"Now I have you, scoundrel!" cried Worthington, aware that flintlocks carried just the one shot. "You will hang for this!"

The highwayman dropped his sack, drew a second pistol from his belt, pointed it at the retired cloth merchant, and fired. A burst of flame, a sharp report, a plume of smoke, and the acrid smell of gunpowder filled the air. Worthington fell backwards.

"Oh my!" gasped his wife.

The scarf fell from his face, revealing a frightened lad, no older than twenty, with a vivid scar running from his mouth to his ear. Panicked, he dropped the pistol, lunged for Worthington's pocket watch and scarpered.

At the King's Arms in Stevenage, servants rushed to carry a groaning Worthington from the carriage, while his flustered wife alternately fussed, wept, and mopped his brow. In truth, it was merely a flesh wound, but Humphrey Worthington was not one to eschew a grand entrance.

Finally, after some 30 miles of tortuous journeying, the inquisitors were alone together. The sun had set and night was drawing in.

Abby had never been so far from London in her life. *The air smells so different out here, so strangely clean,* she thought. When she listened for the familiar city sounds, she heard only the wind in the trees and the cawing of a crow.

The King's Arms was an impressively sized coaching inn, catering to many thousands of travellers the year around. Its timber frames, set horizontally, vertically and diagonally, were painted black, and its wattle-and-daub plastering whitewashed. Its windows, in pairs and threes, bore diamond-shaped leading, and the roofs were tiled in red brick.

Outside hung a large sign depicting King Charles II's coat of arms. Not long ago, the inn had been called The Cromwell, the innkeeper having wisely changed allegiance.

Inside were roaring fireplaces and revelry, smells of roasting meat, hops, pipe smoke and bodily odours. Jacob and Abigail supped on roast breast of mutton and discussed the case.

After a couple of ales, his lingering confidence issues surfaced. "I am but a charlatan, Abigail," Jacob moaned, scratching his head through his periwig. "'Twas you who uncovered the diary thief, not I. I am unsuited to the task: slow of thought and prone to error. Mr Pepys's sister's life may be forfeit if we cannot disprove her witchcraft. The stakes are surely too high."

She raised her eyes impatiently. "Mr Standish, 'tis our combined effort that has brought us here. You have a keen eye for detail and you underestimate your intellect. Only if we face this together can we succeed."

He eyed her sceptically.

Pushing a long strand of red hair behind her ear, she leaned in towards him. "In your absence I'm all but invisible. I can't do this without you."

"Then I dearly hope I shall not fail you, nor Mr Pepys," he replied quietly.


Jacob asked Abigail what she knew of witchcraft, hoping it amounted to more than the snippets he had gleaned from his mentor.

Jacob had been a failed naval purser's apprentice, responsible for supplying the crew with essentials like food and tobacco. Cosseted by his father, he knew little of cunning folk and their familiars. (Sir Miles Standish, Surveyor of the Navy, had recently died in suspicious circumstances. Both Jacob and Pepys believed he had been murdered - a mystery Jacob ached to solve. For now, however, he would give his right arm to solve this one.)

Encouraged by her master, Abigail had read Pepys's copies of King James I's *Daemonologie* and Matthew Hopkins's *Discovery of Witches*. "I know enough," she told him. "But in the countryside 'tis different. There, witchcraft is a way of life. I don't know what we will encounter in Brampton, but I do know the superstition will be strong."

"Do witches frighten you?"

"Not the witches," she replied, pursing her lips.

"You have something you wish to tell me?"

Pausing, Abby shook her head. "Perhaps one day."

Jacob paid one shilling each for their rooms that night, and they slept soundly. The next day, they would arrive in Brampton.

The inquisitors dearly hoped the Worthingtons would not be joining them.

Chapter Three

# To Brampton

Millicent Worthington collared Abigail and Jacob over breakfast of boiled eggs with bread, the mealtime staple. She and Humphrey would not be joining them onward toward Huntingdon, she told them, since he was still recovering from a sore wound and the shock of the attack. The inquisitors feigned disappointment.

"He asked me to give you this," Millicent added, handing Jacob a book.

It was titled *Of Dyes and Dyeing: A Detailed Compendium of the Art and Science of Colouring Fabrics, Containing Numerous Recipes for Dyeing Woollens, Silks, Linens, and Cottons, Intended for the Use of Clothworkers, Drapers and All Persons of a Curious Inclination.*

The author: Humphrey Worthington, Master of the Worshipful Company of Clothworkers.

The onward journey was blissfully undisturbed, though the road surface deteriorated increasingly, causing bumps, thumps and judders.

Abigail tutored Jacob further in the basics of witchcraft, hoping the increased knowledge would boost his self-belief. When she had finished, he took her hand.

"I am much obliged to you, Abigail Harcourt," he told her earnestly. "It seems strange that we knew nothing of one another just two days ago, and now we are inextricably linked."

She squeezed his hand. "Actually, there is something... Since we're to be Master Pepys's inquisitors...," Jacob only fleetingly considered pointing out that he alone had been bestowed the title. "I'd be much obliged if you would call me Abby."

He recoiled in surprise, banging his head on the cab wall and knocking his hat fall off. Grinning foolishly. he retrieved it.

Abigail laughed. "Mr Standish, you are..."

Jacob interjected, "Abig... Abby, if I am to address you thus, then it is only right and proper that you address me as Jacob."

It was her turn to look startled. "Mr Standish, please, you don't understand! In my position..."

But he would hear none of it.

And so our inquisitors became Abby and Jacob.

Shortly after midday, the coach stopped in the picturesque town of Biggleswade, some 20 miles shy of their destination. They took dinner at The Old Bell, a modest thatched inn, where Jacob splashed out on freshly hunted partridge.

The cook had stuffed the bird with seasonal herbs, onion and apple, and served it sliced with a gravy made from the juices. Accompanying the meat were carrots, parsnips and turnip, as well as the usual bread, handy to soak up the gravy. They washed this down with weak ale, as water quality remained dubious, even outside the city.

Although Abby, who had never dined on game before, besides the odd scrap covertly 'rescued' from a Pepys dinner-party plate, found the meat rather rich, she wolfed it down. "If I may be so bold… Jacob? You're a man of some means."

Jacob spooned a vegetable into his mouth. "Upon my father's tragic demise, I inherited a not inconsequential annuity, a testament to his foresight and generosity. He also bequeathed to me a well-appointed townhouse on Strand Lane." He stopped chewing. "He catered amply for my welfare, though I would give it all away to secure his return." Finally, with a gulp, he swallowed.

Sensing his upset, Abby quickly asked, "So you don't need Master Pepys's money?"

"Mr Pepys requested my service and I would never have refused. He and my father were firm friends, and they swore an oath concerning my welfare on my father's death bed. Mr Pepys has kindly become my patron and mentor, which I value far more than any wealth."

"Is your mother still alive?"

"She is, and still resides in Standish Hall in…"

"In Greenwich! I could see it from my quarters when I lived with the Yaxley family! *You're Jacob Standish! One of the Standishes - of Standish Hall!*" She slapped her forehead. "And I call myself an inquisitor!"

Jacob raised a bushy eyebrow and cleared his throat. "Actually… It was not… That is…" He trailed off.

Abby was still admonishing herself. "Perhaps I didn't realise because you don't very much look…"

"Like a gentleman?" Jacob gazed at her apologetically. In his dusty, stained attire, the gangly hulk of a man looked more like a lost child in that moment.


After dinner, they returned to the coach to begin the final leg of their journey. As the gravity of their task set in, the talk returned to witchcraft.

Jacob brought up their previous conversation. "When I asked whether you were frightened of witches…"

"I told you I wasn't frightened of the witches themselves."

"What did you mean?"

She sighed. He had shared personal information with her; it was only fair she be open in return. "Remember our previous investigation, concerning the stolen diaries? We were in a wherry on the Thames, being rowed to Isaac Cornfield's. I told you my father had died in the Clink jail…"

Jacob nodded.

She licked her chapped lips. "I didn't say on whose word he was put there. It was Matthew Hopkins," she said. "The Witch-finder General."

Abby explained that her father, Ambrose, a printer, had distributed pamphlets criticising the 1645 witch trial at the Essex Assizes, advocating reason over hysteria. One had fallen into the hands of Matthew Hopkins, who, outraged, had taken it to his staunchly Puritan ally in Parliament, Sir Tobias Mortimer.

Mortimer, claiming the pamphlets to be a challenge to Puritan authority and the social order, had used his influence to have Ambrose Harcourt arrested. Charged with seditious libel, Abby's father had been found guilty by a judiciary which, at that time, was mired in a frenzy of fear concerning witchcraft.

He was sent to the notorious Clink jail on remand. Mortimer had wanted an example made and again exerted his influence. Owing to the atrocious conditions, Abby's father died of scurvy within a year.

"That frenzy of fear was stirred up by Matthew Hopkins. I lost my home and my father, and it all comes back to him," she said, trembling with emotion. "Now, we face his son."

Abigail knew the Pepys family history well, and she outlined it for Jacob. Her master had been visiting Huntingdonshire since childhood. Samuel's father, whose name was John, was born in neighbouring Cambridgeshire. Pepys Sr moved to London at age fourteen to set up a tailoring business, and sent young Samuel to Huntingdon Grammar School. Via St Paul's School in London and Magdalene College, Cambridge, the bright young man came to the notice of Lord Henry Fairfax through family connections.

Fairfax was the Brampton landowner and a powerful figure in the navy, who saw something in Pepys - keen, resilient, bright - and took him under his wing. As Jacob was to Pepys, so Pepys was to Fairfax.

Pepys went on to work for Fairfax, ultimately leading to his exalted position on the Navy Board. The wealthy landowner also employed Samuel's uncle, Robert, as a bailiff on his Brampton estate, Ravenscourt Manor.

When Robert Pepys died in 1661, five years earlier, Abby explained, he bequeathed his house in the village to Pepys's father, John. (There was some contesting of the Will. Never one to lose out on a delicious windfall,

Samuel, acting as executor, successfully fought off the interlopers and took charge of the property.)

Samuel installed his ageing parents in there, no doubt considering the countryside air preferable to London's smog, and sent his sister, Paulina, along too, to act as their housekeeper.

His mother, Margaret, was a butcher's daughter who gave birth to 11 children, of whom - in an era in which, Abby was keenly aware, fewer than ten per cent died of old age - only four survived. In addition to his sister Paulina, Samuel had two younger brothers, Tom and John.

So he would visit Brampton regularly, to check in on his mother, father and sister, and to visit his mentor, Fairfax. It could not be said that he was close to his sister - he had memorably described her to Abigail as, "not handsome in the face" - yet he clearly felt a duty of responsibility towards her, as the influential elder brother.

He had spent years unsuccessfully trying to marry her off to men he deemed suitable, discovering to his chagrin that she had a mind of her own.

Today, however, as the inquisitors approached Brampton, settling down with a reputable gentleman was the least of Paulina's worries.

Hearing the coach wheels running through water, Jacob poked his head out of the window. "I see only fields and water, not a house in sight," he said.

Their route should have bypassed Brampton and terminated instead in neighbouring Huntingdon. Since they were his only passengers, the coachman agreed to a minor detour on their behalf - for a gratuity, of course.

When finally their coach stopped outside The Bull inn, so aching and stiff were Abby and Jacob's shaken limbs that they practically fell from the cab. "Odd's fish!" exclaimed Jacob, looking up and around. "It is dark and quiet here. I fancy the moon has fallen from the sky."

He was right: it was indeed very dark and quiet at night in Brampton. The modestly sized village was nestled around the 13th-century Church of St Mary Magdalen, which loomed mere yards away from them, and was surrounded as far as the eye could see by flat meadows and woodland.

To Jacob, accustomed to London's claustrophobia, it felt like the middle of nowhere.

The market town of Huntingdon was two miles to the north, and Cambridge was 20 miles south-east. *Might Simon Hopkins already be in Brampton,* Abby wondered, *plying his sinister trade?*

Her master had told her about Brampton. There were windmills and a water mill in nearby Portholme Meadow, she knew, where Master Pepys often strolled when he visited. Many here farmed the land, while others worked as butchers, millers, carpenters, and weavers. It was a microcosm of self-sufficiency.

Candles lit the windows of the two-storey, thatched Bull inn, and a low rumble of activity came from inside. Jacob opened the door for Abby, and, self-consciously, they entered.

All noise ceased, and for elongated seconds the in-habitants - four men around one table; an extravagantly dressed couple, he with a loud voice; a man behind a counter at the far end; a serving maid carrying tankards of ale to another table of three - turned and stared. Jacob noticed the loud gentleman eyeing them particularly sourly.

He removed his hat, nervously twisting it in his hands. "I bid you all good evening," he announced. "I am…"

The man behind the counter appeared in front of him and began furiously pumping his hand. "We know who you are, sir! We've been expecting you, Jacob Standish!"

He was a round-faced fellow wearing a long-sleeved white shirt, brown wool waistcoat and stout apron. He was rather short - his eyes were on the level of Jacob's chest (though Jacob was unnaturally tall) - and he wore a patch over his right eye. This, he popped up and winked with the same eye. Clearly a card.

"Bartholomew Nettlewood, sir. Friends, by which I mean all the village," he laughed, still pumping Jacob's hand, "call me Barty. As may you, sir, since any friend of Sam Pepys is a friend of mine."

The inquisitors noticed he was frothing at the mouth in excitement. It was the first time Jacob had heard his mentor cited so casually.

"And Abigail Harcourt!" he boomed, turning to her. "A pleasure also to make your acquaintance!"

"You know our names, sir?" she queried.

"Naturally! Mr Pepys sent word ahead of you. You are expected. Your rooms are upstairs and your bill for a week's stay is already settled."

Abby and Jacob exchanged looks, shaking their heads in wonderment. Was there nothing he did not think of?

"And Mr and Mrs Pepys?" she asked, referring to Samuel's parents.

"All in good time, my dear. They live in a cottage but a short walk hence," he said, pointing in its general direction. "Tonight, Mr Pepys was firm: you must rest and prepare for an arduous investigation."

Jacob butted in. "Is Simon...?"

Barty smiled, anticipating the question. "Fear not, Mr Standish. We've seen no sign of Simon Hopkins. As I understand it, he remains engaged elsewhere. Though he cannot do so forever."

Weary, hungry, and thirsty, Samuel Pepys's inquisitors settled at a table in the cosy Bull inn, gratefully polishing off a late supper of pottage with bread and cheese, washed down with an ale or two.

# Chapter Four

# Simon Hopkins

*S* imon Hopkins was born in the market town of Manningtree, Essex, in 1646, the year before his father,
Matthew's, death. Although he never knew the man, his mother, Grace, had raised him with the same Puritan zeal and
godliness that her husband had instilled in her. The Puritan
life was a simple one, devoid of luxuries, valuing hard work,
piety and sobriety, shaped by biblical values.

There was one crucial difference between Simon and his
religious kinfolk: his father had been the country's foremost
witch-finder. Feared and abhorred by some, Matthew Hopkins
was revered as a pious, moral crusader by others, having purged
their communities of malevolence. And he was revered no more
highly than in the small household he had left behind.

To Grace, her late husband was nothing short of heroic.


During his early childhood, Simon was home-schooled by
his mother, who taught him to read and write using the Bible
and other religious texts. Later, he received a basic academic

*education within the local community, where fellow pupils began to find him aloof and distant.*

*Aged 14, he was enrolled in his father's alma mater, Emmanuel College, Cambridge, known for its godly and Puritan leanings. There, he began to stand out, for the intensity of his debate and for the questioning of his tutors, concerning what he considered to be doctrinal impurity. Some counselled that he would do well to temper his fervour.*

*Outside of lectures, he would admonish fellow students for their behaviour, as a self-appointed moral guardian. Peers began to shun him, and he appeared not to care.*

*An incident the year before his graduation almost led to his expulsion. A fellow student, Elias Whitmore, like Hopkins a loner, kept in his room a black cat, which he would talk to. The pair fell out over a minor religious dispute and Simon accused Elias of witchcraft, alleging the cat to be his familiar.*

*The resulting furore led to an internal investigation, which found Hopkins's allegation baseless. He received a severe reprimand and final warning.*

*His final dissertation was titled: 'A Puritan Discourse on the Wiles of Witchcraft - Exposing the Threat to Godly Society and the Path to its Eradication'.*

*Many, both tutor and student, were glad when he left.*

*With a classical university education  behind him, Simon Hopkins could have become an academic, authored religious texts, or entered the legal profession. He chose none of those paths.*

*Since a very young age, Simon had dreamed of but one thing: following in his father's footsteps. Seeking out evil wherever it plied its heathen trade, identifying and eradicating it. It was his fervent desire to keep alive his great father's memory, though many would prefer to forget – and to reaffirm Matthew Hopkins's righteousness.*

*He knew full well that the journey would be a hard one. The role of witch-finder had lost much of its status since his father's day, and he embraced that. It excited him.*

*After spreading word that he would continue his father's godly work, he set out on horseback in the summer of 1666, from Manningtree to Cambridge. He was 20 years old, only seven years younger than his father had been when he died.*

*This would be his second investigation, the previous one having ended unsatisfactorily with the acquittals of the accused. But he was learning his trade. Slowly, slowly, catch a witch.*

*In this latest matter, a mother and daughter, Sarah and Prudence Sawyer, had been accused of witchcraft by their neighbour, the cattle farmer, Henry Drayton. Drayton's wife, Lucy, had refused Sarah a cup of milk, and the old woman had been heard to curse under her breath as she left. That night, Lucy Drayton had fallen ill with a fever and within a week had died.*

*In the aftermath, Sarah and Prudence had allegedly been seen holding a witch's sabbat, in which they summoned their familiars and suckled them, praising the Devil.*

*These were grave allegations, and Simon Hopkins's attire bore testament to that. He wore a broad-brimmed hat with a tall crown; a cape fell down his back and his doublet was paired with a wide linen collar that lay flat over his shoulders. His bucket-top leather boots, fitted with spurs, were made for riding. All were in muted shades; no hint of embellishment or embroidery. He also wore riding gloves and carried a long wooden staff.*

*It was one of his father's outfits. With his long, raven-black hair and beard, he looked so much like his father, his own mother could barely have told them apart.*

---

# Chapter Five

# The Pepys Household

The inquisitors awoke at dawn. Jacob had sunk one too many ales the previous night and was hungover.

Their rooms were simply furnished and rustic. Both had a wooden four-poster single bed with heavy woollen covers. Candles lit the room at night, along with an oil lamp on a bedside table. A small fireplace in each room had warmed the space prior to their arrival. Embroidered wall hangings, depicting village life, provided a decorative touch and helped keep in the heat.

Abby unpacked her bag and transferred its contents to a chest of drawers, then washed herself using the supplied water jug and wash-basin.

Jacob went to do the same and remembered he had not had time to pack. He caught his reflection in a looking glass and shuddered. Stubble had grown haphazardly about his young face and his pale-blue eyes were

dark-rimmed. He noticed a dried blob of something -
mud, he hoped - above his left eye and scraped it off.

Abby opened the shutters and gazed out at a sight
she had never witnessed before. A rich reddish sun was
shining over the horizon, and verdant hues stretched out
before her. Greenwich, where she had lived for a while
with relatives, had boasted many sizeable gardens, but
this was something else. She opened the window and
breathed in the air. It was so wonderfully fresh, nothing
like the smokey, ordure-ridden stench of London.

A cow called out in the distance, and there was warmth
on her face.

She would like it here in Brampton, she decided.


To her left, Abigail spotted a row of cottages, in the
same direction that the innkeeper, Barty, had pointed the
previous night. *Do John and Margaret Pepys live with their
daughter, Paulina, in one of those?* she wondered.

Abigail and Jacob breakfasted together in the Bull's
tap-room, where they had feasted the previous night.
They ate porridge sweetened with local honey, accompa-
nied by fresh, plump plums and blackberries. When they
had finished, a floppy-eared brown-and-white dog wandered in and sat beside their table, demanding attention
and eyeing their leftovers.

Last night's serving maid, who turned out to be Barty's
wife, Harriet 'Hatty' Nettlewood, called the dog's name

– "Rusty!" – and shooed it away. Then she joined them at their table.

Hatty was twice her husband's size, bosomly with apron, and wore a cotton headscarf over tied-up chestnut curls. Her cheeks stood out like rosy apples and her voice was thick with catarrh.

Though they were the only souls in the room, she spoke in a husky whisper. "What did Barty tell 'e last night?" she asked, leaning in conspiratorially. Her thick rural accent was unfamiliar to the inquisitors.

"I beg your pardon?" asked Jacob.

"What did 'e learn last night?" Hatty repeated, only louder, then looked around to see if anyone was listening in. They were not.

"What did he learn last night?" Confused, Jacob turned to Abby. "Does she mean me?"

The innkeeper's wife regarded him as if he were simple, and Abby laughed. "'Tis a countryside dialect, Jacob. She means, 'What did you learn last night?'"

When he still looked confused, she laughed and slapped him playfully on the arm.

Hatty seemed taken aback at such familiarity from a servant girl. Abby's face reddened and she apologised, then was quiet for some time, brooding.

So it was Jacob who explained what they had learned from Barty over supper.

His recollection of the conversation went like this…

Actually, there were two women accused of witchcraft in Brampton: Paulina Pepys and her friend, the clothier, Rebecca Thacker. Samuel was either unaware of this or purely concerned with his sister's welfare. Jacob believed the former; Abby suspected the latter.

Rebecca cut fabrics and sewed them to produce bespoke country attire for men and women. Since Paulina was a herbalist, the two had started an unusual joint venture selling herb-infused clothing, which they claimed had health benefits: enhancing the mood, uplifting the spirit, and curing headaches.

Their accuser was a local crop farmer, Godfrey "Goddie" Grimston.

Goddie, who was often drunk, one day stumbled into Paulina and Rebecca's clothing stall at the weekly Brampton market, muddying items and breaking jars of their herbs. The women swore at him and made threats. The next day, Goddie accused them of casting a spell that had summoned a hailstorm – "Stones the size of apples!" he had claimed - which had badly damaged his corn crop, losing him a significant sum of money.

Then the following night, on his doorstep, he found a poppet: a woven doll figure in his likeness, with a pin through its heart. It was made from straw and lavender stalks. Remembering the women's curses, and aware they used lavender in their clothing business, he was certain it had come from them: a witch's calling card. Since then, Goddie claimed, he had lived in fear of being murdered in the night.

"To anyone who would listen, he would rant about Paulina and Rebecca being witches, that they should be made to pay for their crimes," said Jacob. Seeing Hatty shake her head in disgust, he added, "Your husband did assure us that Grimston was a troublesome type, and always up to trickery."

"Aye," Hatty agreed. "Many didn't believe his nonsense."

However, as Jacob recalled Barty telling them, a substantial number of credulous souls in fear of witchcraft surely did.

It had seemed that the incident might blow over - until the local magistrate, Bulstrode Bennett, became involved. He had taken Goddie's accusation very seriously indeed, riding personally to Manningtree to call on the services of the witch-finder, Simon Hopkins.

Finally, Abby found her voice. "After Barty finished telling us all this, there was an incident," she said. "A loud, smartly dressed gentleman, who'd been drinking wine with his wife, stopped at our table on his way out. He told us that he knew who we were, and that we weren't welcome in Brampton."

"According to Barty, that was Bulstrode Bennett," said Jacob.

The recollections concluded, the innkeeper's wife folded her stout arms. "My husband do love his gossip and tells a fine tale. Ain't nothing more I can add."

"We must go and speak to Mr Pepys's sister," said Abby.

Jacob raised his finger. "Mrs Nettlewood, I wondered… Do you have any spare clothing that I might borrow? Mine is long-travelled and rather…"

"Stinking?" suggested Hatty.

He grimaced. "I was inclined to say 'soiled'. Though now you mention it…"

Hatty pointed out that her husband's clothing would be several sizes too short for Jacob. "Try the Pepys girl's friend," she told him. "Clothing's her business. She'll find something for 'e."

John Pepys's house was indeed in the row of dwellings Abby had seen from her window. It was barely a ten-minute walk from The Bull, following a footpath that skirted meadowland.

Functional yet quaint, it was a two-storey, timber-framed, lime-plaster building with a tiled roof dominated by large chimneys. Set before it were flower and herb gardens, with cherry trees and a summerhouse.

While she and Jacob were still some small distance away, a young woman flung open the front door and came running out to greet them. The hem of her house-coat billowed behind her as she ran, its collar flapping wildly.

"Mr Standish! I'm so happy to see you!" she called out.

Paulina Pepys - for it had to be her - practically bowled Jacob over as she hurled into him and clung on, like a drowning woman clinging to flotsam.

Noticeably uncomfortable at such over-familiarity, he tentatively returned Paulina's gesture.

Suddenly aware of her social faux pas, she let go, stepped back and curtseyed. "Please forgive me," she said quietly. "I have awaited your arrival with great anticipation."

Twenty-six years old, she had a pale complexion and freckled cheeks. Her dark blonde hair was pulled back and covered in a white linen cap. As she stood there, finally sensing support after the growing anxiety of the witchcraft allegations, she began to cry.

Jacob looked about to run away, so Abby stepped forward and put a hand on the young woman's shoulder. They had never met before, although her master occasionally spoke of his sister.

Paulina withdrew sharply. "I need no solace from a serving girl, thank you," she snapped, instantly all out of tears.

Abby's mouth fell open. She was aware that Pepys had installed Paulina in his own house, prior to her time in his employ, as a maid. *Does it still rankle?* she wondered. "I'm here because your brother entrusted me to help Mr Standish," Abby pointed out.

Paulina glared at her. "And I fail to understand what assistance you could possibly offer."

*It clearly does still rankle,* Abby realised.

As Jacob stood stiffly, unsure what to say, he felt something wrap itself around his ankle. Leaping up onto one foot, he looked down to see a white cat staring up at him, its erect tail twitching.

"Be gone, Sugar!" Paulina scolded the creature, and it darted off towards the summerhouse.

At least the incident had broken the tension.

Upon entering the house, they found themselves in the hallway. The ceiling was considerably lower than in Jacob's townhouse, and he smacked his forehead on the door frame.

Samuel Pepys's parents stood stiffly side by side, awaiting their introductions. John and Margaret Pepys were in their mid-60s, now living a quiet life. Both had grey hair, his receding and hers largely covered by a bonnet. It helped that their doting son had provided for them a comfortable place to live, in the open country air, and that he paid towards their upkeep.

Mr Pepys Sr wore a trimmed goatee and sharp attire befitting a former tailor: a well-cut doublet over a linen shirt with a wide collar, silk stockings, and brass-buckled leather shoes diligently waxed.

Mrs Pepys looked similarly elegant in an understated way. She wore a linen smock beneath a lace-trimmed gown, featuring fitted bodice and billowing skirt. It had detachable sleeves. A kerchief was draped around her shoulders and tied at the neck. Her leather shoes, similarly waxed, were laced.

Their outfits were charmingly, if eccentrically, colour-coordinated. Both wore ochre outer garments, a bright yellow undergarment and tan leather shoes.

But their worn and lined features told a less glamorous story. Their faces were pallid, with sunken cheeks and dark-rimmed, squinting eyes.

"Mr Standish," said John, bowing slightly. "We are most indebted to you. And to you, dear Abby."

Abby shot Paulina a look and the Pepys woman scowled back.

"Sam speaks highly of you both, and we pray you conclude this lamentable matter swiftly," John continued. He motioned for them all to be seated at a large table in the centre of the room. "Thus we must turn our attention to the Grimston oaf and his ungodly, baseless aspersions."

"Wicked man!" exclaimed his wife. The words stuck in her throat, she coughed, and John gently patted her back.

The walls and timber-beamed ceiling were plastered and whitewashed. A portrait of Samuel gazing proudly hung from one wall.

Leaded windows, three abreast, allowed wide shafts of September sunlight in. The large brick-and-timber fireplace would not require lighting until the evening.

The inquisitors repeated the facts of the story as they understood them. Paulina, pointedly addressing Jacob whenever she replied, confirmed that Goddie Grimston had indeed been drunk when he had wrecked their market stall, and that it was true, she and Rebecca had threatened him - but of course they were empty threats, uttered in the heat of the moment.

The young woman was barely holding it together. "Mr Standish, you must believe me, I am no witch," she pleaded. "Grimston is well known for his falsehoods and takes perverse delight in the misery of others."

John slammed his fist down on the table. "Goddie Grimston is a fabricator and a simpleton, sir!"

His ailing wife was overtaken by a coughing fit.

Jacob did not know where to look.

Abby addressed Paulina. "Why do you think Goddie singled out you and Rebecca?"

Paulina sighed and looked to her father.

"Paulina, if Sam places his trust in Abby then we are bound to do the same," he told her gently.

His daughter huffed petulantly.

Abby straightened. "When is Simon Hopkins's arrival expected?" she asked innocently.

At the mention of the witch-finder, Paulina's face crumpled and she began sobbing. As Margaret moved in to comfort her, Abby blushed.

John put his head in his hands. "Oh, this is a grave matter. If the young Hopkins is anything like his father, we must brace ourselves for dark and sinister dealings."

This only heightened his daughter's anguish and she ran from the room followed, hobbling, by her mother. Their footsteps were heard heading upstairs, then clomping across the ceiling above.

When all fell silent, Abby asked again why Goddie chose to single out Paulina and Rebecca, of all the women in Brampton. John Pepys confessed that he was at a loss. Half the village had cause to avenge the wayward farmer's slights and misdemeanours, he said, for which Goddie might then seek retribution. But why his daughter?

"I dearly wish I knew," he confessed, "for it might help us to refute the foul slander." Then suddenly a spark came into his eyes. "Hold! I recall now… When Grimston first cast this slander, it was Paulina alone whom he accused. Only on the following day did he also name Rebecca Thacker. That I found curious indeed."

"Mr Pepys?" asked Jacob.

The old man cocked his head.

"I do greatly admire your attire, sir," said Jacob.

Abby shot him an incredulous look.

Fortunately, like his son, Pepys Sr was not immune to flattery. "I am obliged to you for your kind words, Jacob. Our garments were commissioned from Mistress Thacker this past summer. We have donned them continually since, as they are greatly admired among the villagers. The cut is excellent and the colours matched with some skill. However - I beseech you, sir, speak nought of this to her, for she is quick to take umbrage - I believe the girl did charge me overmuch."

Jacob opened his mouth to speak, but the old man had not finished.

"I would have taken needle to fabric myself," John said, then sighed. "Alas, my eyesight fails me."

"Indeed, sir, I am in dire need of fresh attire and was curious as to who had crafted yours," Jacob explained.

John chuckled. "I see, Jacob. I have no doubt that Mistress Thacker can accommodate your needs. She is most adept, even for gentlemen of your tall stature."

Before leaving, Abby asked John Pepys whether they could have a final word with his daughter. More than anything, she wanted to see Paulina's living quarters.

There were three rooms on the ground floor - hall, kitchen, parlour - and three bedrooms upstairs, one for each occupant. The old man directed them towards the furthest door.

Abby gestured for Jacob to knock. This time, mindful of the low frame, he stooped to enter.

The scents that greeted them - rosemary, lavender, sage, thyme, mint, too many mingling for the nose to single out any particular one - sent them almost giddy.

Dried bunches of herbs hung from the wooden beams, others grew in pots on window sills. Labelled jars on shelving and in cabinets occupied one wall, and there was a work bench beneath the window, ranged with tools that glinted in the sunlight.

One wall was lined with bookshelves, while an oak bed with a simple bedside table stood beneath a tapestry depicting the four seasons.

It was a tidy space, filled with homeliness and personality.

Abby was quietly impressed. "You're a herbalist," she said.

Paulina's face was expressionless. "What of it?"

"All these jars of herbs and potions. A witch might be said to live here," Abby pointed out.

"She has lavender hanging there," said Jacob. "The same herb that was used to make Goddie Grimston's poppet."

Paulina buried her face in her hands. "What are you implying? Do you also accuse me of witchcraft? My brother's inquisitors?"

Abby felt a pang of sympathy for the wronged woman. "Nay, Paulina! Only that your work may fuel Simon Hopkins's flights of fancy, and that we must proceed with great caution."

# Chapter Six

# Rebecca Thacker

Paulina's friend and business colleague, Rebecca, lived at the other end of the row of dwellings on which the Pepys's lived. It made sense to pay her a visit first, although questioning Goddie Grimston was clearly urgent.

Rebecca's house was smaller than the Pepys's and had a sign hanging outside:

**Rebecca Thacker – Clothier**

Before they knocked on her door, Abby stopped and signalled for Jacob to do the same. The sun was high in the sky and the gnats were biting. They seemed to favour Jacob, perhaps drawn to a stronger odour.

"Jacob," Abby said. "You told me 'twas of the utmost importance that you personally succeeded in our investigation."

He nodded.

"Then you must stop becoming distracted! When Mr Pepys tells us important information, please do not reply, 'I greatly admire your attire'!" She could not help giggling.

Jacob tugged on his periwig. "The gnats are biting me," he said sulkily.

Rebecca Thacker, beaded in sweat, looked as pleased to see Jacob as Paulina had been, although she stopped short of hugging him. "Come in," she urged, beckoning. "Please, come in." She, too, had been expecting them.

Once again, the scents of herbs and herbal concoctions were overpowering (and made Jacob realise he ought to buy a few plants for his own house, to mask some of his more manly odours).

The lower floor was divided, half serving as a workshop, the rest as a living area.

Rebecca, however, was nowhere near as tidy as her business partner. The workspace was covered in piled rolls of material and crumpled remnants of cloth, in so many different colours. Scissors, a yardstick, pins in pin-cushions, needles and so much more were scattered across a work bench. Finished garments hung from pegs on the walls.

Pots, jars and brushes were strewn about the floor, and a large blue stain, likely dye, marred the wooden floorboards. A dressmaker's dummy, clad in the beginnings of a green doublet, had fallen over by the window, and an iron was heating over a fire in the hearth. The room was rather too warm.

The living area fared little better, with pots and pans piled on a table, and dirty plates poking from a ceramic wash-bowl.

Rebecca noticed the inquisitors surveying the room with barely disguised horror and laughed. "There are scarce enough hours in the day," she explained. "Would that I had a husband to help with the tidying."

"But you don't?" Abby asked.

"'Tis a small village, Brampton. The choice of men is dire." She laughed ruefully. "There was once a gentleman… He died in the war."

"Paulina is unmarried also?" asked Abby, though her master had already told her as much.

"She's courting Will Farlow, a clerk from Huntingdon. They're to be married soon," replied Rebecca.

"When?" asked Abby.

"At the end of this month. The date was moved forward at Paulina's request, after the witchcraft allegations were made, in case…," the clothier trailed off.

"Is this Will Farlow a gentleman?" asked Jacob.

Rebecca's laugh was heavy with irony.

"You don't approve?" Abby asked.

"What's it matter if I approve?"

When neither inquisitor replied, the clothier shrugged. "It appears to me that he covets the name Pepys more than he does her. But she won't hear of it."

Rebecca Thacker exuded the no-nonsense air of a woman who worked hard. She was barefooted and her hands and apron were stained with dyes of various colours. Her fingertips, Jacob noticed, were covered in tiny wounds from all the needlework.

Asked about her craft, Rebecca told the inquisitors that she made clothing for patrons as far afield as Cambridge, such was her growing reputation. The fabrics, she bought in from local cloth merchants, then created, cut and sewed her own designs. She had been experimenting with blends of dyes to formulate new colours of clothing that she hoped would become fashionable among her wealthier clients.

Her reputation had, of course, taken a tumble since Goddie Grimston's accusations, and orders had fallen off significantly. People did not wish to be associated with a witch.

The question remained as to why Goddie had singled her out. Abby mentioned the incident at the market stall: the altercation and the threats.

"'Twas Paulina who ranted at him and called him names," Rebecca claimed. "If anybody should be accused of witchcraft, it is her, not I."

"*You blame Paulina?*" Jacob exclaimed.

"I do," she replied firmly. "And when Simon Hopkins comes, I shall tell him so."

The inquisitors shared a glance.

"Mistress Thacker, I believe it best to act together to fight these baseless accusations," Abby told her. "To divide would be to give Hopkins the upper hand."

"I tell it as it is," Rebecca replied, folding her arms.

"What may we do to affirm her innocence?" asked Jacob.

Abby had to stop herself from congratulating him on his new-found directness of questioning.

Rebecca threw her arms in the air. "Goddie Grimston's crop was laid low by hailstones, not by witches!" she exclaimed.

Yet a significant number of locals believed Grimston, Abby pointed out, including the influential magistrate, Bulstrode Bennett. How on earth were they to disprove it? An act of God versus an act of the Devil?

Before they left, Jacob brought up his need for fresh clothing. Rebecca told him she had a few items that might fit him, a gentleman of a similar size having recently cancelled an order. So while Abby perused the jars on Rebecca's shelving, Jacob sifted through her stock, gratefully picking out a linen shirt and breeches, and a pair of plain wool stockings.

Keen to divest himself of his grimy old outfit, he disappeared upstairs to put them on. When he returned, Abby burst out laughing.

"You chose the same colour undergarment as Mr and Mrs Pepys!" she pointed out. "You're trying to flatter them!"

Jacob reddened, yet he did not deny it. "The shirt is a tad tight," he replied.

"I'll still want paying, Mr Standish!" insisted the clothier. "For the three garments my price is two pounds and ten shillings."

Jacob furrowed his brow. "Dear lady, I envisaged the amount would be less than a pound!"

"Take it or leave it," she replied firmly. "My garments are the finest in the county."

"Little wonder Mr Pepys bemoaned your prices!" Jacob blurted out, instantly recalling that John had urged him not to mention that particular bone of contention.

Abby regarded him askance.

"Mr Pepys did what?" Rebecca demanded, glaring.

Chapter Seven

# Goddie Grimston

A bby and Jacob took dinner back at The Bull, where they collected their thoughts over plates of fish pie, filled with pike and perch taken from the nearby River Ouse.

"We can't prove that hailstones weren't summoned by witches," Abby said. "But we could prove that Goddie Grimston concocted his allegations. If that is true - and we must trust that it is, for my master's sake - then the question is: why? In revenge for some trivial matter, we are told."

"Their rantings after he drunkenly damaged their wares at market?"

"Yet Rebecca claims it was Paulina who ranted and that she's the witch. 'Tis troublesome."

He nodded pensively.

"Our path is clear," said Abby. "We must speak urgent-ly with Goddie himself."

The innkeeper's wife, Hatty, directed them to a smallholding on the outskirts of the village and warned them, "Beware that Goddie Grimston - 'e's touched in the head."

A path leading away from the Pepys's home took them past rows of thatched cottages. As usual, Abby had to double-time to keep up with Jacob's lengthy strides.

When bystanders spotted them, they would confer conspiratorially, as if Mr Pepys's inquisitors were known and distrusted throughout Brampton. It gave them a general sense of unease.

Still, the sky was cloudless and the gnats seemed to trouble Jacob less since he had changed his clothing. The terrain was generally flat, and boggy in places. The sprawling Nuns' Meadow lay to their left, and to their right, the larger Portholme Meadow. Both were dotted all over with colourful wild flowers. Sheep and cattle grazed there, and the sails of windmills could be seen turning in the breeze. Maids were out in the fields, milking the cows.

Ahead in the distance, they could make out a grand manor house set among ornamental gardens.

"That'll be Ravenscourt Manor," said Abby. "Where Lord Fairfax lives with his wife, Lady Eleanor. We may need to speak with him, since he holds sway over all these lands."

"*Speak with Lord Fairfax?*" exclaimed Jacob. "He would never countenance such a thing!"

"We're Master Pepys's personal inquisitors. He and Lord Fairfax are firm friends." She tapped the side of her nose. "It matters not what you know, but more who you know."

Jacob harrumphed and looked appalled.

They turned left at the stile beneath the oak tree, as instructed. It took them down a dry mud track beside a stone wall. Ahead was a farmhouse surrounded by crop fields bound by hedgerows. Distant figures were working in one field, harvesting. Sheaves of hay were piled in another field, and beyond that, what looked like an orchard. Far away, on the horizon, lay clustered woodland.

The Grimston farmhouse was a single-storey stone building with a thatched roof. Its window frames had oiled fabric stretched over them. *These people cannot afford glass*, Jacob thought to himself.

Before he could knock on the interestingly warped front door, it opened. Jacob stumbled backwards in shock. A woman stood before them, and they caught the distinctive odour of baking bread coming from inside.

"You must be the so-called inquisitors who're the talk of the village," said the woman. "Pleasure to make your acquaintance. I'm Anne. Goddie's wife. For my sins."

"Is he in?" asked Jacob.

She was a striking-looking woman, he noticed, beneath her evident poverty. She had piercing blue eyes and plaited blonde hair, pinned at the back of her head. Although her dress had been mended in several places and her apron was covered in flour, he sensed a fierce, dignified spirit.

Stepping past Anne and into the farmhouse, he saw an oven and loaves on a table by a fire; shelving was lined with jars of ingredients and herbs hung from rafters. One section of flooring was covered in straw and neatly piled blankets - a makeshift sleeping area, Jacob surmised. It was a humble, well-tended space that commanded his respect; hardly the domain of a heathen, which he had expected. The tantalising aromas of cooking made his stomach rumble.

Suddenly, he felt himself tugged back by the farmers wife, with a ferocity that took him by surprise. *These farming folk are surprisingly strong,* he mused. *Even the women.*

"My Goddie's not in there," Anne told him brusquely. "He's out in his fields, harvesting." Then, out of the blue, she grasped Jacob's forearms and stared pleadingly up into his eyes. "Promise me you'll save the Pepys girl!" she implored him.

It took Jacob by such surprise that he became dumbstruck.

Abby stepped in. "You don't believe Paulina Pepys is a witch?" she asked.

Anne shook her head firmly. "Nay, not at all. Do you believe she'll hang?"

Abby found herself seriously considering the prospect for the first time. "Nay," she replied, with more conviction than she felt inside.

Jacob, buoyed, added, "We shall clear her name and be gone by the morrow!"

Anne narrowed her eyes. "'Tis not the word around the village."

"No person has been harmed, only crops," Jacob assured her. "Even if she is found guilty, she will not hang."

Anne finally releasing her grip on Jacob's arms. "I'm pleased to hear it. That young woman is no witch."

"You'd swear the same to Simon Hopkins?" asked Abby.

"'Tis not my place to say, my dear. Who'd listen to a farmer's wife? My fool husband and magistrate Bennett, they're the ones."

"Where may we find your husband?" asked Jacob.

"In the field below, with my three sons, harvesting the barley."

"How will we know him?" he asked.

"Don't you worry about that," Anne replied. "You'll know him."

As they approached the barley field, a man they assumed to be Goddie Grimston came charging towards them. He was carrying a pitchfork and bellowing, "Nay! Nay! I know who you are!"

Abby and Jacob eyed each other nervously.

"What should we do?" he asked.

Goddie ran at him, pitchfork prongs aimed at Jacob's midriff. Deftly for someone his size, Jacob tackled him around the ankles, then pinned Goddie's arms with his knees and tossed the pitchfork aside.

Goddie's head resembled a sunburned turnip: round, ruddy, and with thinning straw-coloured hair sticking straight up from his scalp.

"Leave me be!" he yelped. "I'll tell the magistrate!"

Even from his lofty position, Jacob could smell the beer on the farmer's breath. "But it was you who assaulted me," he pointed out.

"It matters not. Mr Bennett's coming for you," snarled Goddie.

Abby tugged on her fellow inquisitor's shoulder. "Let him go, Jacob."

"She knows," said the farmer, sneering, revealing gums where teeth should be.

Jacob realised they had become surrounded by three men, his age and younger, with the hardened physiques of manual labourers. Goddie's sons, no doubt. None of them spoke a word; their glowering expressions did all the talking. One brandished a sickle, another a flail, while the third clenched his fists.

"We should leave," said Abby.

Jacob eyed each of the gnarly Grimston boys in turn and nodded. Better to retreat and live to fight another day, just as his father had taught him.

The Grimstons jeered as the inquisitors left.

"I know what I saw!" Goddie called after them. "Your precious Mr Pepys's daughter will hang!"

# Chapter Eight

---

# Hopkins's Arrival

Simon Hopkins pushed bitter memories of Cambridge academia from his mind as he entered the town's boundary. The ride from Manningtree had taken three days, passing through Colchester, Halstead and Haverhill. The summer had been hot and August's roads and tracks – most commonly, compacted mud – were in a reasonable condition. Only in some of the more rural outposts had his jet-black horse, Jeremiah, slipped or stumbled.

He passed through the town, with its mix of stone and timber-framed buildings, churches and inns, where merchants, townspeople, students and scholars mingled. Horse-drawn carts passed him, heading in the opposite direction. Market traders were selling fish and meats, bread and ale, textiles and tools – all manner of goods for the burgeoning area.

Hopkins sighted the ominous Gothic architecture of King's College Chapel, then crossed the River Cam. There, urbanity gave way to more picturesque scenery, as people rowed small *boats on the water. He sneered at openly cavorting couples, promising them Hell and damnation under his breath.*

*Around mid-afternoon, he reached his destination, a small hamlet on the north-west outskirts of Cambridge. Brampton, his next port of call, once business here had been satisfactorily concluded, was just 20 miles away. A brace of witches had been reported there, and their time would surely come.*

*Two dozen or so timber-framed houses with thatched roofs had smoke curling from their chimneys and a flickering glow in their windows. Animals - sheep, cows and chickens - in nearby enclosures called out. The only other sound, besides the clip-clop of Jeremiah's hooves, was that of a blacksmith in his forge, nestled beside a tributary of the Cam, hammering away at metal. Beyond, stretched fields and woodland.*

*Hopkins spotted an inn with a sign: The Blacksmith's Inn. He was pleased to see a Norman church nearby, made from local stone with a tiled roof, although he disapproved of its central stained-glass window, believing its gaudiness distracted from the true faith. Within its grounds was a small graveyard.*

*All was peaceful and bucolic, for the present.*

*A middle-aged man in a long, filthy smock, appeared in one of the doorways, bustled towards the witch-finder, stopped and bowed. His feet were bare, his nose was bent and his face was pock-marked. "Mr Hopkins?" he asked. When Simon nodded, he added, "You look like your father, sir."*

Hopkins, who had been taken aback by the man's pathetic appearance, glowed with pride. Not only had he achieved his desired effect, but a peasant knew of Matthew Hopkins, even down to his abiding features.

His horse, Jeremiah, snorted, perhaps registering the man's pungent odour, and Hopkins dismounted.

"Henry Drayton?" he asked.

Drayton nodded, which he turned into another bow.

"I come on behalf of God, to remove from this land the foul pestilence of devilry," Hopkins told him, smiling at how it sounded.

He had waited his entire life for this moment – to serve the Lord and avenge the slurs and injustices his father had endured. Such a righteous path, to uphold the same virtuous pursuit! Let them come at him! He was serving God; his detractors lacked moral fortitude.


If the stench of Henry Drayton had been bad enough in the open air, the inside of his hovel's was overpowering. Cattle smells mingled with those of unwashed clothing and sour milk, bodily odours with those of a shaggy dog drooling in one corner. It was clear that the recently deceased Goodwife Drayton had been responsible for the housework.

A rat scurried out from beneath a sack of animal feed and fled the house.

"Forgive the mess," Henry said, and Hopkins laughed for the first time in years.

*He should have felt bad about it - all were God's children, after all - but he did not.*

*A fire was going in the hearth, over which a cooking pot had been suspended. A straw bed lay at the opposite end. A rickety table and two stools sat before the fire.*

*Placing a handkerchief over one stool-top, to protect his breeches from stains, Hopkins sat down and bade the farmer recount all he knew concerning the Cambridge witches.*

*Drayton began weeping almost immediately. The tears created a glistening path through grime on the poor man's cheeks. He recounted the incident concerning the cup of milk: how his wife had refused Sarah Sawyer's request - the pair having argued the previous week over an unpaid cheese bill - and had heard her mutter something as the door was closed, which she believed to be a curse.*

*"That very same night she fell ill, sir, on that very bed," Henry told him between sobs. "Shaking and vomiting, such as I'd never seen. Speaking in tongues, she was, cursed by them witches. I tended to her as best I could, but she grew only worse. A week later, my wife Lucy was dead, at the hands of Sarah and Prudence Sawyer, sir."*

*"Pray, what is thy proof that these women are witches?" Hopkins asked, aware that he would need cast-iron evidence to present to the local magistrates, with whom he was unfamiliar.*

*"I saw them, sir, the very same night that my dear Lucy died. In a copse over yonder. Cavorting naked, they were, with the*

Kipling girl. A witch's sabbat, such as I had heard tell of, but never thought I would see with my own eyes."

Hopkins's eyes gleamed. "There were three witches, thou sayest?" A veritable coven. The evil in this hamlet ran deeper than he had thought.

"Indeed, sir. Each did call to their imp, and the terrible animals came. I remember their names, sir!"

They were: Prickears, a black rabbit (Sarah Sawyer's familiar); Dainty, a tiny black kitten (her daughter Prudence's); and Pluck, a brown mouse (Dorothy Kipling's).

"They danced in a circle, praising the Devil, then suckled their imps, who disappeared from whence they came, sir. A most terrible sight. I thank God I was not seen by them."

Having finished his tale, the farmer slumped, exhausted.

"God is merciful," said Hopkins. "But he shall show no mercy to these abominable sorcerers. 'Thou shalt not suffer a witch to live.' Let us pray and give thanks together, Henry Drayton. And that tomorrow I may succeed in bringing these foul demons to justice."

Chapter Nine

# Incident at Supper

I t had been an illuminating, if frustrating, first day of investigation for the inquisitors. If they had hoped to manipulate their main suspect towards a confession, through the sheer weight of Mr Pepys's influence, they now knew they were sorely mistaken. An uneducated farmer, Goddie Grimston may have been; easily cowed, he was not.

All that tied Paulina Pepys and Rebecca Thacker to the charge of witchcraft were Goddie's accusation and the fact that both women worked closely with potions and herbs, which were the witch's stock in trade. This evidence, such as it was, was flimsy at best.

However, Abby knew the methods of the witch-finder: let the evidence mount while confounding the minds of the accused. If one alleged witch could be turned on another - which appeared already to be happening in Brampton, even before Simon Hopkins's arrival - then the upper hand was gained.

Hopkins could offer Rebecca Thacker immunity if she joined the prosecution. Then Paulina Pepys would be on her own - the Brampton witch.

A wise and balanced magistrate might quell the rising hysteria, dismiss the witch-finder's so-called evidence, and consider the facts objectively. That is how many accused women had escaped the noose, or had even been found innocent of all charges and the case thrown out of court.

From what the inquisitors knew, Brampton did not have a wise and balanced magistrate. It had Bulstrode Bennett.

The situation was serious indeed.

Having freshened up in their rooms at The Bull, Abby and Jacob were shocked to find Goddie Grimston seated with his wife in the tap-room. The farming couple were washing down bread and cheese with beer while playing cards.

Immediately the farmer saw them he rose from his stool, sending it toppling backwards. He marched towards them, weaving unsteadily on his feet, clearly inebriated.

As Jacob stood to confront him, Goddie pushed a doll made of woven straw and herbs into his face, shaped like a man. A pin pierced the figure where its heart would be.

"See this!" he shouted, slurring. "The witches' curse on me, which they delivered to my door. The pestilent agents of Satan are at work, but I will have justice before they strike."

"The poppet could have been left at your door by anybody in this village," Abby countered.

"Smell it!" ordered Goddie, thrusting it towards her.

She obeyed, not wishing to rile him further.

"Lavender!" Goddie declared, belching. "Such as the Pepys girl uses in her daily trade. The woman is no herbalist. She's a witch!"

The tap-room had fallen very quiet; everyone present was transfixed by the scene. How would Mr Pepys's inquisitors react to such a display of aggression, from one so far beneath their purported station? Word had spread throughout Brampton that they were the finest inquisitors in the land. One circulating rumour suggested that they had, on one occasion, been commissioned by the King himself.

In the event, Mr Pepys's inquisitors reacted with stunned silence.

They were saved by the innkeeper, Barty, who was accustomed to confrontations among his customers. Although he was half the size of the hulking, vegetable-headed farmer, he strode forward and pointed towards Goddie's table, where his wife Anne was still sitting, head down, embarrassed.

"Be seated!" he ordered him.

Leering, Goddie shoved the poppet into Jacob's hand and snarled, "You keep this. Maybe the witch's curse will find you next."

Goddie Grimston was far from the simpleton John Pepys had described. He was a dangerous adversary with powerful allies. If Abby or Jacob had hoped they might breeze through the case - and they surely had in heady moments - they were now fully disabused of the idea.

They took a table as far from the Grimstons as the tap-room would allow, only to realise they were seated just two tables from Bulstrode Bennett and the woman they assumed to be his wife. Once again, the couple were dressed in unnecessary finery for a meal at a local inn, and his booming voice rose high above the crowd's general murmur.

So the inquisitors were grateful for the distraction when Hatty Nettlewood appeared at their table, to take their order for supper.

"Didn't put Goddie Grimston in his place, did 'e?" she said, folding her arms.

Jacob's gratitude vanished, and he stared into his ale.

"'Tis but our first day in Brampton, Hatty," Abby replied. "We do well to avoid making a scene."

Hatty looked unconvinced.

Both inquisitors were aware that they dare not lose the confidence of the locals. Word of mouth and gossip spread fast in rural communities. Winning them over would be a powerful tool against Simon Hopkins. The alternative did not bear thinking about.

Jacob spoke up. "See this." With some effort he reached in beneath his new shirt, which clung too tightly to his chest, and extracted a thin gold locket. Abby had never noticed it before. It was finely engraved with a family crest and was clearly an expensive, exquisite piece of work. "This was given to me by Mr Samuel Pepys, in gratitude for my retrieval of his stolen diaries. Inside is a miniature portrait of Mr Pepys himself. A keepsake he gifted me."

Abby kept her counsel, knowing that Master Pepys had done nothing of the sort.

Hatty leaned in, cooing. "May I touch it?"

Jacob hastily pushed the locket back inside his shirt. "Nay, you may not," he told her. "We hunger. Bring us your finest supper! And quickly!"

Hatty tipped her cloth cap and bustled away, apologising as she went.

In a whisper, Abby asked Jacob, "Who gave you the gold locket?"

He pulled it out again and showed her the picture inside.

"Your father, Sir Miles?" she asked.

"'Twas given to me on the occasion of his death."

"You tricked her."

"I did indeed."

A sudden commotion drew their attention.

Goddie Grimston had fallen backwards off his stool and lay convulsing on the floor. His body juddered as he waved his arms manically in the air, as if fending off imaginary flying beasts. Anne began screaming hysterically and Barty, who had been standing at their table, bent over Goddie's thrashing figure, uselessly repeating his name.

The inn's patrons craned their necks, then began edging closer to watch. All beside Bulstrode Bennett and companion, that is, who were engaged in an argument the inquisitors could not help overhearing, concerning his wastage of food.

A man in a plain dark-blue doublet pushed through the crowd, carrying a buckled leather bag. On noticing him, the onlookers willingly parted, murmuring to one other. The local physician, thought Abby.

Goddie's convulsions having ceased, he lay on his back with his hands shaking, wreathed in sweat.

"'Tis the witches' curse!" someone cried, to murmurs of agreement.

The physician knelt, took Goddie's pulse, and lifted his eyelids to inspect his pupils. "Goddie? Goddie?" He spoke calmly, but received no response.

The farmer began mouthing wordlessly, frothing at the lips.

The physician reached into his bag, sifted through its contents, and pulled out a stoppered bottle of brownish liquid. "Fetch a cold compress!" he called out. "And a blanket!"

As Barty and Hetty Nettlewood busied themselves with these orders, the physician tried pouring the liquid into his patient's mouth. Goddie merely spluttered, and the tonic being administered dripped uselessly down his cheek and onto the floor.

The physician returned to his bag, seeking an alternative treatment.

Goddie lifted his head off the floor, bloodshot eyes wide, staring into space. "The b...," he groaned.

It was his final mortal utterance. His head fell back and he lay motionless.

The tap-room fell eerily silent, broken by Goddie's wife's awful cry of anguish.

A voice piped up, "What did he say?"

"The b-something," replied another.

Bulstrode Bennett rose from his table, his chair scraping loudly across the floor, drawing all eyes to him. "The Brampton witches!" he announced with practiced authority. "Those were the words Goddie Grimston sought to speak, ere death's cruel hand clutched his heart. *The Brampton witches.*"

"They've killed him," said Anne Grimston, barely audibly, before crumpling to the floor in a faint.

While a couple rushed to help her, the physician closed Goddie's eyelids, so no one need witness his expression of terror any longer.

Jacob felt something in his pocket and pulled it out. It was the poppet Goddie had thrust upon him.

Had the witches indeed struck?

# Chapter Ten

# **Aftermath**

T he death of Goddie Grimston necessitated a sharp turn in the investigation. Suddenly, the inquisitors were not merely defending Paulina and Rebecca against accusations of witchcraft; since their accuser was now dead, allegedly at the hands of witches, they were now defending potential murderers. The courts would take that very seriously indeed.

Goddie had been silenced – at least, that was how it appeared. Add witches' curses and dark magic, and the cauldron of fear was being vigorously stirred.

"If Paulina and Rebecca didn't kill Goddie, then who did?" Abby wondered out loud. "And why?"

The most obvious answer was, they agreed, to throw more suspicion on the two women and to escalate the seriousness of their alleged crimes.

"What if they are indeed witches?" asked Jacob.

Goddie's body had been taken home, trailed by his inconsolable wife, to await burial. The inn had cleared quickly afterwards, its patrons all out of appetite after the awful scenes they had witnessed. Only Abby and Jacob remained.

"Do you believe in witchcraft, Jacob?" Abby asked.

He was still clutching the straw poppet, as if it had become attached to him through its unearthly powers. He shuddered. "I confess, it is not easily dismissed in my mind. Many tales and accounts have reached me, which are too strange to fathom. How else can one explain the grim misfortunes that plague us? How does one adequately explain the demise of Goddie Grimston?"

Abby prised the poppet from Jacob's grip and sniffed it. "Lavender indeed," she said, tucking it into her coat. "I've spoken with Master Pepys on the topic of witchcraft. We've delved into the literature and share the same view. The world is full of enigmas that defy explanation; he leans towards rational, scientific explanations over demonic forces. And I concur. We must consult the physician who treated Goddie in his final moments. His perspective will be rooted in science."

Jacob looked thoughtful. "If science is indeed at play, then any man present might have brought about Goddie's demise. Though I confess, the method escapes me."

Abby nodded. "Any man - or woman - precisely, Mr Standish. We must compile a list of suspects. Our best chance of proving Paulina and Rebecca's innocence is to find out who killed Goddie Grimston. We'll interrogate everyone and see who lies. Goddie's death and the witch-craft accusations must be linked."

They were seated at their table in the darkened tap-room, just a candle between them shedding flickering light, all other oil lamps and candles having been extinguished. It felt intimate, almost spiritual.

Hatty had retired to bed, but her husband could still be heard bustling about in a back room. Jacob called to him, and soon Barty appeared at their side, wheezing.

"Would you join us?" Jacob asked.

Barty pulled up a stool and slumped onto it, exhaling wearily. He had removed the fake eye-patch and, in the dim light, the bags under his eyes seemed deeper than ever. "Oh dear oh dear oh dear," he exclaimed, all out of his customary good humour. "Such a terrible sight. It will do nought for my custom."

"Nor for Anne Grimston's livelihood," Abby added.

"Indeed, it goes without saying. And that poor man."

"Did you like him?" Abby asked.

Barty patted her arm. "Nay, not at all. Precious few did. Should we sup an ale?"

When the innkeeper returned with three pewter tankards and set them on the table, Abby quizzed him further. "You said that few folk liked Goddie. Might any wish him dead?"

"Where to begin?" came the reply.

The inquisitors waited for laughter, a sign that he was joking. None came.

Barty listed those present in The Bull during the incident, who had some connection to the investigation. Abby pulled a quill, ink-horn and notebook (donated by her master) from a pouch attached to her belt, and wrote them down.

*Bulstrode Bennett (and wife, Helen) - the magistrate*
*Will Farlow (seated with Lord Fairfax's stablemaid, Alice Wilkins) - Paulina's suitor.*
*The physician, Archibald Bramwell - attempted to treat Goddie.*
*Anne Grimston - Goddie's wife.*

"Is that everybody?" Abby asked.

"Ah!" Barty exclaimed, slapping the table for effect. "Mistress Thacker was here but a short while before you arrived. She was returning my favoured doublet, having mended it."

*Rebecca Thacker*

Abby frowned as she added the name to her list. "That's the last thing we need. The very woman we strive to exonerate, here present ere Goddie's demise."

"Surely you don't suspect her?" the innkeeper asked.

"She sought to blame P…" Jacob began to reply.

Abby placed a finger to her lips, silencing him. "Best we keep our counsel, Jacob."

It riled Barty. "The good folk of Brampton have a right to know if there's a witch in their midst," he snapped. "Did you and I not witness the same terrible events? Consider the poppet Goddie thrust upon you, Mr Standish, the like of which he found before the ruin of his crop. That was witchcraft, plain and simple."

Abby smiled to herself. The credulity of these country folk was only to be expected. It was her task as an inquisitor to seek a scientific explanation for these supposed occult occurrences. And to discover who had good reason to see Goddie dead.

She addressed the innkeeper. "You said that Will Farlow dined here with Alice Wilkins. Yet Farlow is Paulina Pepys's intended?"

Barty took a healthy slug of ale and licked his lips. "Farlow and Wilkins were once betrothed. But when Paulina showed interest in Farlow, he quickly switched his affections. As you may imagine, Mistress Wilkins took great offence."

"Yet they were together here on this night," Abby pointed out.

Barty leaned forward, beckoning them to do the same. "I cannot know what takes place in others' chambers. Nor would I wish to," he told them, ignoring Abby's sceptical look. "However, I do know this. Mr Farlow is audacious, while Mistress Pepys is all too innocent in the ways of love."

"Did they leave the inn together?" Jacob asked.

Barty paused, considering the question. "Amidst all the commotion, I could not say for certain... May one of them may have murdered Goddie?"

Abby, who had not yet met either Will or Alice, shrugged.

"They are not witches!" Barty exclaimed.

"Witches, Mr Nettlewood, take many forms," Jacob replied. "They are known to mislead and to disguise themselves in order to avoid suspicion."

Finishing her ale with a flourish, Abby set down her tankard. "Or perhaps the truth lies outside these tales of witchcraft? Jacob, we should retire to our beds. Tomorrow we pay an early visit to the physician, Bramwell - and we shall need our wits about us."

# Chapter Eleven

---

# The Good Physician?

Archibald Bramwell, being Lord and Lady Fairfax's personal physician, was afforded his own quarters in a wing of Ravenscourt Manor. He advised them on hygiene and performed regular bloodletting to balance their humours, which was believed to promote good health.

He had also overseen the birth of the couple's ten children - most efficiently, it should be added, given that not one had died in infancy.

The previous day's glorious weather felt like a distant memory as Abby and Jacob set off towards the Ravenscourt estate, following a nourishing fresh-fruit breakfast. Initially they followed the route to the Grimston farmhouse, having spotted the manor house the previous day.

The sky was uniformly grey, one looming raincloud, and a low-lying mist blanketed the ground in all directions. It was chilly and faintly drizzling, though neither inquisitor seemed to mind. The damp brought out the scent of sweet, wet grass, which made a welcome change from London's stench.

Jacob was nervous, far more so than Abby, who had grown accustomed to meeting the rich, titled, and entitled in her daily life of servitude. Her master often hosted high-ranking navy officials, rich merchants and assorted hangers-on at Seething Lane, where she would help serve the food, ensure the guests' comfort, and still maintain a low profile. Pepys dearly loved to entertain, and to be entertained.

"I dread the thought of meeting Lord Fairfax," Jacob told her, head bowed, scuffing his leather soles like an errant child. "I am sure to be tongue-tied and make an utter fool of myself."

As he looked up, a horse-drawn cart emerged through the mist in the distance. A shadowy figure led the horse, pulling a cart laden with hay. Distracted, he tripped over a dead branch in his path and toppled sideways into a ditch.

"Mr Standish, whatever are you doing?" Abby asked.

Wordlessly, he brushed himself down and returned to the trackway.

The old farmer leading the cart eyed Jacob suspiciously as they passed. "Saw you jump into that there ditch."

"I did not jump," Jacob replied sulkily. "I tripped."

"Oh aye," said the farmer. "From London, are ya?"

The road dipped and took them over Alconbury Brooke via the stone-built Nuns' Bridge with its five wide arches. Ravenscourt Manor's magnificent gatehouse lay ahead.

Jacob nervously inspected his doublet, which was now muddied from his fall. He licked his hand and rubbed frantically at a stain. "I shall require fresh garb once again," he muttered to himself.

Abby skipped ahead, turned to face him, and walked backwards, swinging her arms. "That would be a shame, since I so greatly admire your new shirt." Her tone suggested a quip was coming. "It makes you look like a Pepys!"

She ran off, laughing, as Jacob chased after her. Both, in that moment, forgot all their concerns, which would return soon enough.

The stone gatehouse boasted a vast arched wooden door, large enough for a horse-and-carriage, with smaller arches either side for pedestrians. The main door was conveniently open, with no guard in place - Lord Fairfax clearly expected no trouble. The parapet was crenellated, hinting at fortification. Above the main arch were intricate carvings of floral motifs and two stone guards holding cut tree trunks, all bearing a Gothic influence.

It reeked of wealth and prestige.

Once through, the sight that beheld Abby and Jacob was yet more spectacular: Ravenscourt Manor itself. As a regular visitor and friend of the esteemed owners, her master had often boasted to her of its history.

The house - more of a palace, given its size - had been built in the 11th century and was once a Benedictine nunnery, hence the Nuns' Bridge over which the inquisitors had recently passed. Oliver Cromwell's ancestors had taken over the estate the previous century, following its requisition by Henry VIII during his persecution of Roman Catholics. It had subsequently passed into the hands of the Fairfaxes. Queen Elizabeth and King James had both stayed there.

The grandeur of the grey stone architecture left the inquisitors awestruck. Enormous bay windows to the left of the main entrance would allow light to flood into the grand halls within. The roofline cast a jagged silhouette against the sky, with chimneys, triangular gables and further crenellations.

A circular lawn to the left of the driveway, bisected by a tiled pathway, was dotted about with manicured topiary. Further into the distance, flower and herb gardens could be seen growing.

To the right of the main building, perpendicular to its walls, was another vast section built in contrasting red brick, a reminder of the continual evolution of the manor house. Behind that, further rooftops were visible, suggesting the estate went on forever.

"Could we not return to the inn?" Jacob asked, tugging on his periwig.

A servant opened the main door to them, and bowed. "How may I assist you?" he asked.

The interior smelled of wood and beeswax, and they could make out a grand dark-wood foyer with intricate carvings and portraiture adorning the walls. The ceiling was such a height as they had never before witnessed.

The servant was tall, almost Jacob's stature, though twice his age, wearing forest-green livery with small pewter buttons and a silver family-crest pin in his lapel. Respectful yet wary, he introduced himself as Edgar.

Jacob waited for Abby to speak, as was his wont. When she did not - it was hardly a housemaid's place, even one now playing inquisitor - he stammered, "We are here on behalf of Mr Samuel Poop... nay, Pope!"

Edgar raised an eyebrow haughtily. "Pope, sir? I do not believe we are acquainted."

"Mr Pepys!" exclaimed Jacob, reddening. "Mr Samuel Pepys! The Pope would be another fellow entirely. Forgive me, I am an ass."

"Indeed, sir," agreed the servant, somehow making it sound polite.

Once assured of their credentials, Edgar led them outside and around the main building to yet another vast wing of the estate. Pointing to a door, he told them, "The physician, Bramwell's quarters."

"Is Lord Fairfax in residence?" Jacob couldn't help asking.

"His Lordship is in London, sir," replied Edgar.

"Oh thank God!" Jacob blurted out, then threw a hand across his mouth, horrified. "I mean…"

"I know what you meant, sir," the servant intoned witheringly, and flounced away.

When he was out of earshot, Jacob buried his face in his hands. "Why did you allow me to speak?" he groaned.

"Come!" said Abby, leading the way to Bramwell's oak door. "I'll do the talking, fear not."

Archibald Bramwell's face was instantly recognisable from the night before. He smiled readily, exuded warmth, and was rather handsome, Abby considered, if a little old for her tastes (he looked to be in his late forties). He was also perhaps the cleanest man she had ever met.

He had long, perfectly manicured fingers and a clean-shaven face, though his grey-tinged hair was casually tousled. His clothing, too, suggested he was not one to stand on ceremony. His cravat hung loosely, and his emerald-green velvet coat had seen better days.

"Pray enter," he said. "We shall sit beside the fire that you may dry your garments. I noticed you both at The Bull last night, witnessing Grimston's tragic demise. I

gather you must be Mr Pepys's well-regarded inquisitors?"

"Most seem to welcome Goddie's demise," said Abby,
ignoring his question.

Bramwell squinted at her curiously. "All men are created equal…? I do not know your name."

"Abigail. Abigail Harcourt."

He bowed, took her hand, and kissed it. "All men are
created equal, Abigail," he said, fixing her gaze.

"And I, sir, am Jacob Standish. Also inquisitor to the
esteemed Mr Pepys."

Bramwell barely acknowledged him.

They were in a spacious room that appeared to be
part-study, part-living-area. Stained-glass windows all
around cast multiple swathes of colour delightfully about
the interior. An oak desk was strewn with papers and
books, while the table beside it was topped with all manner of apothecary equipment: mortars and pestles, bottles
and jars, containing herbs, powders and liquids. Books
lined the walls.

The physician bade them sit on a well-worn sofa with
plentiful cushions, and took a seat in the armchair opposite. "How may I assist you?"

"In your opinion, what caused Goddie Grimston's
death?" Abby asked.

Bramwell laced his fingers together and smiled. "By
which you mean, do I believe in witchcraft?"

Abby said nothing, but merely fixed his gaze.

The physician continued. "We cannot discount any means of death, mortal or otherwise. However, I am a man of science and am inclined to more pragmatic solutions. The human body, while complex, often reveals its secrets to those who know where to look. It is these secrets – not the whispers of superstition – that guide my judgments in matters of life and death."

He allowed the statement to linger, enjoying the inquisitors' evident impatience for answers.

Jacob could no longer contain himself. "And what is your professional opinion, sir?"

"I would not care to speculate."

"You believe the man was poisoned," stated Abby.

"I do," Bramwell replied.

Jacob gasped, grasped Abby's arm, noticed he had done so, and let go.

"Why do you believe he was poisoned?" she asked.

"The dilation of his pupils," he explained. "The poor man's violent agitation. However, the cause of death may be by another method entirely. We cannot discount witchcraft."

"What was the liquid you administered to him at the inn?" asked Abby. "I noticed Goddie died mere moments afterwards."

Bramwell burst out laughing. "I do admire a woman who speaks her mind!"

"And the liquid?"

He stopped laughing and stared at her. "It was a tonic of my own concoction. Chamomile, peppermint, rose hip and willow bark, in a base of brandy."

"What was your hope for it?"

"I hoped that it might cure him. As we saw, it did not."

"Might you, sir, have cause to wish Goddie Grimston dead?" she asked.

Jacob harrumphed, appalled at her mounting audacity. "I do beg your…"

Bramwell interrupted him. "Hush, Mr Standish. It is an apt question for an able inquisitor. However, my answer is nay. Now, pray, allow me to make us some tea!"

The moment he left, Abby leapt up and began inspecting the physician's supplies, turning bottles to inspect their labels. Jacob could only watch in horror. *No one should rifle through the personal effects of a man of such distinction,* he thought.

Bramwell's voice rang from another room: "If you seek poisons, Abigail, allow me to spare you the effort. I possess many, each employed in my research of medical treatments."

Sheepishly, she retook her seat. Jacob glowered at her, his disapproval unmistakable.

"Foxglove may be used to treat heart conditions and dropsy," Bramwell explained as he returned with a silver tray of expensive porcelain cups. "Hemlock may be used for spasms and arsenic as a general health tonic." He set the tray down. "In small doses."

"Which do you believe killed Goddie Grimston?" chipped in Jacob, clearly fascinated.

"I could not say."

"What if I were to ask the same?" said Abby.

"Then I would reply, belladonna."

Jacob's mouth fell wide open.

Bramwell went on, regardless. "In my practice I am well acquainted with its symptoms, which include dilated pupils, hallucinations and convulsions, such as Grimston exhibited."

"Do you, perchance, keep belladonna, sir?" asked Abby.

"Aye, I cultivate the same and indeed experiment with many poisons. Any reputable physician would do so," he replied, pausing for effect. "However, you should remember that, in the form of the plant deadly nightshade, belladonna grows wild in English hedgerows. Its berries are as black as night. Look carefully, and you will find them in Brampton."

They sipped their tea. Abby had never tasted the drink before, it being an expensive luxury, and she found it strange and bitter. After all the talk of poisons, feeling paranoid, she left her cup largely untouched. Jacob, accustomed to higher circles, was familiar with both tea and coffee - another exotic import, which had become increasingly popular among London's men of business - though he far preferred ale.

Talk turned to Goddie's final utterance: "The b..."

"It may well be as the magistrate, Mr Bennett, stated that night: 'The Brampton witches'," Bramwell suggested. "As far as I am aware, the farmer fervently believed in their existence."

Abby adjusted the hem of her dress. "However, he might also have been saying..."

"'The beer'," cut in Bramwell.

"We must speak with Barty Nettlewood concerning his cellar," she told her fellow inquisitor.

As they departed, Jacob asked the physician whether he knew Alice Wilkins.

Bramwell appeared momentarily unsettled. "Naturally. Why do you ask?"

Jacob explained that they knew the stablemaid worked on the estate, and they needed to talk with her. (He did not add that he preferred to ask the rude physician for her whereabouts, rather than the pompous servant, Edgar. Both had made him feel small; one smaller than the other.)

Abby was more blunt. "You seemed surprised by the question?"

"Alice Wilkins is noted for her volatile temper and possesses... a certain reputation. A man of my standing finds it prudent to avoid her company." He opened the door for them. "Mr Standish. Abigail Harcourt." His gaze lingered on her. "I trust you will honour me with another visit. Perhaps next time in a less professional capacity."

# Chapter Twelve

# The Stablemaid

L ord Fairfax's stables were a good half-mile from the
  physician's quarters, yet still within the sprawling
estate. Though the mist had lifted, a fine drizzle persisted.
The inquisitors passed through ornamental gardens, laid
out geometrically, as well as kitchen- and herb-gardens.

Jacob noticed a cluster of plants bearing shiny black
berries. Deadly nightshade, he felt sure, and he wondered
aloud, "Bramwell's poisons?"

Sheep and cattle were dotted about the yellowing,
sun-dried fields and orchards, and water meadows were
visible in the distance. Grazing horses, gathered in a
fenced enclosure beside a wide, low slate-tiled stone
building, signalled their destination.

Alice Wilkins was inside, in one of a dozen stalls,
grooming a muscular black horse with a white forehead
and fetlocks. Other horses, fine specimens used by Fairfax
for hunting, peered from their stalls, curiously eyeing the

visitors. The pervading bouquet - new to Abby and Jacob - was distinctive: hay and straw mingled with manure.

So engrossed was the stablemaid in her brushing that she did not notice the inquisitors watching her, their arms resting on the gate of the stall. Both were accustomed to horses, from the hackney coaches of London. Never had they encountered a beast as majestic as this one.

"May I stroke him?" asked Abby.

Startled, Alice let out a gasp and swivelled to see where the voice had come from. Instantly, she was in Abby's face, thunder in her eyes. Fearing she may be physically assaulted, Abby recoiled, and, as quickly as it had risen, the stablemaid's rage vanished. The rapid mood-change was as disturbing to Abby as the initial threat had been.

Before she knew it, Jacob was between them, squaring up to the stablemaid. Although he was significantly taller, Alice looked as powerful as the thoroughbreds she handled.

Abby pulled him gently aside. "'Tis fine, Jacob. I'm sure we can speak civilly?"

"That depends. Who in the blazes are you?" the stablemaid demanded.

"You wear perfume," said Abby, noting the scent of sandalwood and mint that had enveloped her.

"What of it?" Alice retorted. "It masks the odours of the stable."

When they were finally introduced and the stablemaid was comfortable with their credentials, Alice opened the gate to join the inquisitors. As she did so, Abby moved to approach the horse.

Alice shot out an arm, barring her way. "No one touches Lord Fairfax's horses," she growled. "Only myself, the stable master, and Lord and Lady Fairfax. Lest there be dire consequences."

Abby had intended to begin boldly, asking about the stablemaid's night out with her former fiancé – Paulina Pepys's supposed suitor – Will Farlow. Since that now seemed unwise, she asked instead about her history with the Fairfaxes, to break her quarry in gently.

Alice informed Abby that her father, John, was the current stable master, and that his father, grandfather and great grandfather before him had all looked after the horses on this estate, dating back to the 16th century. They discussed the estate and her duties, and Abby mentioned that they had just come from Bramwell's.

Having lulled her into a false sense of security, the inquisitor began in earnest. "You were at The Bull inn last night – the night of Goddie Grimston's death?" (A question, not a statement, though she already knew the answer.)

Alice, however, was equal to it. "You know I was. You were there."

Abby was about to reply when Jacob butted in: "Aye, with Will Farlow!"

The stablemaid exploded not with rage, as Abby had anticipated, but with hilarity. It took a while for her to calm herself. "Is that what you think? That I lay with that goat, Will Farlow, when he is intended for the sister of your Mr Pepys! Oh my!"

She returned to her grooming, careful to close the gate behind her. "He wishes to rekindle a fling that was as brief as a candle's flicker. Thus, he offered to pay for my supper. I would not share his bed again, were he the last man on this earth. And I told him so."

"I can imagine you did," Jacob muttered to himself.

"Who do you believe caused the death of Goddie Grimston?" Abby asked.

"How would I know?" Alice grunted with exertion while she brushed. "I groom horses and clean out their mess. I'm no witch-finder."

"You believe his death was the work of witches?"

The stablemaid shrugged. "'Tis what Goddie said."

"You were friends with Goddie?"

She stopped brushing and straightened up. "Has somebody been talking?"

Since they had not - at least not about Alice Wilkins - the stable fell silent, but for the snuffling of the animals.

"Who is it? Who has spread lies about me?" Alice snarled.

No one had.

She went on, clearly seething. "It couldn't be Archie Bramwell…"

Jacob coughed, quite innocently, having inhaled an airborne mote.

"What's he said?" The stablemaid advanced on them once again.

Jacob held his ground, motioning for Abby to stand behind him.

"I presume he told you how Goddie Grimston trampled over his prized herb garden? How he destroyed a precious plant vital to his research?" Reaching the gate, Alice kicked it hard. "How he flew into a rage and threatened to have him dispatched?"

Jacob shook his head. He had not.

Abby poked her head out from behind Jacob. "What about you, Alice Wilkins? Would you wish Goddie dead?"

The stablemaid jabbed Jacob's chest. "Wish Goddie Grimston dead? She asks me if I would wish that dullard fool dead?" Suddenly, her mood changed. Something had crossed her mind that upset her. A single tear escaped Alice's eye and she turned around, ashamed of her distress.

As the stablemaid regained her composure, a story emerged.

Goddie Grimston had been employed by Alice's father, she told them, to supply hay and straw for the estate's horses. He was unreliable, tardy, prone to drunkenness, and often delivered fewer than the agreed-upon number of sheaves. One day the previous year, exhausted of patience, Alice's father had fired him on the spot.

That same night, someone - though everyone knew precisely who - wedged open the stall-gate of Lord Fairfax's favourite horse, Shadowmane. The horse escaped the estate grounds, escalating a frantic search the following morning, only for the poor creature to be found lifeless in the river.

Fired by rage, Fairfax used his influence over Magistrate Bennett to force Goddie into court. Alas, the evidence was merely circumstantial.

The strongest punishment that could be handed out, in due application of the law, was a fine and a public apology. Fairfax declined the apology, still seething.

Alice and her father were fortunate to escape with their livelihoods, thanks to the family's generations of service.

"I value horses more than men," Alice concluded bitterly. "But I could not extinguish a man's soul, not even one as dark as Grimston's."

"Did you trust her?" Jacob asked Abby, as they made their way back to the village.

"I don't know who to trust," she replied. "Why do you ask?"

Jacob stopped walking. "Did you the delicate silver chain around her neck? And the finely embroidered silk handkerchief tucked into her belt?"

Abby stopped also. "I did not. You're suggesting…"

"That such items would be beyond a stablemaid's pay."

"She has another source of income?"

Jacob shrugged.

Puzzling silently, they continued onward.

# Chapter Thirteen

# Will Farlow

It was mid-afternoon by the time the inquisitors reached The Bull, weary yet buoyed by their achievements. The grey clouds had disappeared, replaced by a pale sunlight.

Their interrogations had been largely successful. Goddie was likely poisoned, they had learned. The physician - though he had concealed the fact - had reason to do away with the farmer, as did the stablemaid, who had been more forthcoming.

It was more than they could have hoped for, so early in their investigation, the housemaid and the failed purser's apprentice.

Although the interrogations had been predominantly Abby's, Jacob felt some pride. He may not have contributed the lion's share, but these were early days in his new career - as Mr Samuel Pepys's personal inquisitor, no less - and he felt he was learning fast. Certain insights had surely been his, he considered… After all, had he not coughed at that moment, Alice Wilkins would never have blurted out Archibald Bramwell's motive for murder.

He would repay Mr Pepys's trust in him yet.

Before they ordered food, and both were starving, the inquisitors were keen to quiz Barty Nettlewood. If Goddie had indeed been served poisoned beer - the scientific method of dispatch - then who had served him? Might the jovial innkeeper himself have been the one?

Come to think of it, Abby realised, she had omitted his name from her list of possible suspects, as well as that of his wife.

*Barty Nettlewood*
*Hatty Nettlewood*

When Barty arrived at their table, he closed his eye not covered by the fake eye-patch. Flailing his arms around, his fingers found Jacob's face and began tracing the outline of his nose. "I cannot see, sir!" he wailed. "I am blinded!"

"Try swapping over your patch, sir," Jacob suggested.

The innkeeper did so, closed the exposed eye, and continued his charade. "It is no use, sir! Spare a shilling for a blind man!"

"*Mr Nettlewood!*" barked Abby, instantly curtailing the alleged hilarity.

Unfortunately, the innkeeper's testimony only muddied the waters. He had personally served Goddie and Anne Grimston's beer, he told them. He had filled a jug from a barrel behind his counter, then refilled their tankards directly from that, standing at their table.

He recalled the Grimston's being in good spirits - she having bartered her baked goods for the drinks, so they cost nought - and that they had toasted his good health, both drinking the same decanted brew.

"Goddie died; Anne did not," Barty concluded. "It is not possible he was poisoned."

Abby screwed up her eyes and rubbed her chin. "You saw them both drink?"

Barty nodded.

Jacob raised his finger. "What if…?" he trailed off.

"Please, Jacob, continue," she urged, open to any theory.

Jacob was keenly aware that he would likely embarrass himself. "I do not understand the science of poisons," he said. "But I wonder… Is there a poison that does not act immediately? Which takes effect only after a delay?"

Abby's face lit up. "You're suggesting the poisoned beer wasn't the one poured by Barty at the table, but a prior drink he had already consumed? So anyone present might have added the poison to his brew?" She turned to

Barty and asked, "Did Goddie partake of more than one beer?"

"You saw him yourself. He drank several."

Jacob tugged his periwig down over his forehead. "I do apologise, I am…"

"No, Jacob! You have it!" She grasped his hand across the table and shook it delightedly. "Goddie Grimston was already poisoned when Barty poured that draft!"

"Pray, lower your voice!" Barty hissed. "All this talk of poison is bad for business!"

A hand slammed down onto the table between them, with such ferocity that their tankards jumped. All three looked up to see an unshaven young man, his face contorted with drink and ire. In his other hand he held a clay flagon that seemed empty.

"I hear I am the talk of Brampton!" he announced, spittle flying from his lips.

Barty rose and placed a firm hand on his shoulder. "Calm yourself, Will Farlow, or I shall have to throw you out."

Farlow pushed him to the floor. "You and whose army, little fat man?"

Jacob stood, looming taller than Farlow. "Pray, Mr Farlow, sit with us," he said. "We will explain."

Jacob could see his addled mind turning over.

Hesitantly, Farlow sat. "Bring me cider!" he ordered Barty, pushing his flagon at the innkeeper. "And be quick!"

The fresh alcohol seemed to raise the young man's spirits, and Jacob wondered whether it was a lack of cider, rather than learning of their investigation, that had made him so irate. One thing was for certain: in Brampton, word very quickly got around.

Farlow appeared to have taken a tumble: his long waistcoat was ripped, his right cheek grazed, and his breeches were filthy. Yet his twinkling blue eyes exuded a ready charm. To Abby, who had met his sort before, he looked like trouble.

"Why have you been asking questions about me? Who are you?" Farlow demanded.

He was the first person in the village not to know who the inquisitors were… Then they remembered: he hailed from Huntingdon, the neighbouring town, two miles away.

When Jacob explained their purpose in Brampton, it did little to quell Farlow's suspicions. "What has that to do with me?" he demanded to know. "I've never met this Goddie Grimston."

"He's the man accusing your paramour, Paulina - my master's sister - of witchcraft," Abby explained. "And now he is dead."

Farlow rolled his eyes. "What of it?"

"The witch-finder, Simon Hopkins, may be riding to Brampton as we speak," said Abby.

"What business is that of mine?"

They were getting nowhere.

Out of the blue, Farlow drunkenly shoved Jacob's shoulder. "Who's this lump? Can he not speak?"

The inquisitor glared at him. "Aye, I can speak. So answer me, Will Farlow: Where did you sleep last night?"

"With Alice Wilkins, with whom you dined on the night of Goddie's death?" Abby added.

Farlow smirked. "Aye," he replied, laced with sarcasm. "I lay with Alice."

"She says you did not," Jacob countered.

"Everybody lies."

"Do you lie, Will Farlow?" Abby asked.

With a wink, he replied in a stage whisper, "I laid with Paulina Pepys."

"I do not believe him," said Jacob. "Paulina's father would never countenance such a thing."

"Who are you people?" Farlow retorted, slurring. "On whose authority do you interrogate me?" Rising, he up-ended his flagon into his wide-open mouth and guzzled down the dregs, though plenty of it splashed down his shirt-front. With a dramatic flourish, he wiped his mouth with the back of his sleeve. "You will, pray, excuse me? It is a long walk back to Huntingdon."

Farlow staggered out of The Bull and into the chill Brampton night.

# Chapter Fourteen

# Hopkins's Witch-Hunt

*S* *imon Hopkins spent the night at The Blacksmith's Inn, where he watered and fed his horse, Jeremiah. He made no friends there, a chill presence, sitting alone in a corner. Over the course of the evening, he nursed a single small ale – which parents gave to their children, as a healthier option to the water – with which he swilled down a bowl of pottage.*

*The inn itself comprised a single tap-room on the ground floor with – Hopkins noted with approval – simply furnished guest rooms for travellers above, offering merely a straw mattress and a woollen blanket.*

*A wood fire in a hearth and scattered oil lamps lit the downstairs space. There were a few tables and stools for patrons, and plain tapestries were hung on the walls for added warmth.*

*The landlord and his wife ran the place; he was stationed behind a counter, she bustled about serving a handful of travellers and locals. Both of them seemed to know who Hopkins was, suggesting that word had spread, and they treated him* warily, clipped in their conversation and averting their eyes. He enjoyed their fear.

As he prepared to retire for the night, when the sun sank beneath the horizon around eight o'clock, an incident occurred.

Two men seated together had clearly journeyed from London, as evidenced by their loud conversation, which had only grown louder as the beer flowed. When their talk turned to the theatre, one stood and began dancing, singing as he did so, and slopping his beer over the straw-strewn floorboards.

Hopkins had not wanted to cause a scene – he preferred to keep a low profile until the time came to strike – however his patience had reached breaking point.

He stood, bolt upright, pointing his staff at the drunkard. "Cease this heathen display at once!" he bellowed.

The dancing man stopped and stared in shock at Hopkins. Squinting, he sized him up. He was bigger than Hopkins – and drunker. Seeing the other man's Puritan garb, and perhaps recalling the tyrannical years of the Commonwealth and Oliver Cromwell, the arch Puritan, he spat on the ground.

Although Hopkins's upper lip betrayed the slightest of twitches, he held his ground. He had never had a fight in his life, although he had caused a few. "I demand a public apology forthwith," he announced. "Such moral degradation shall not be tolerated in a godly society."

The drunkard took a step forward; Hopkins took a step back. The landlord appeared and spoke to the drunk man quietly. "Don't mess with that man. Apologise to him and be seated."

*When he did not acquiesce, but still eyed Hopkins men-*
*acingly, the landlord added, "Please."*

*Eventually, deliberately, the drunk man obeyed, all the*
*while eyeing his accuser.*

*Hopkins smirked and demanded they all pray, in atone-*
*ment for such outrage.*

*It was a tense prayer.*


*Sarah and Prudence Sawyer lived in a thatched cottage*
*on the edge of the hamlet. Since Sarah's husband, John, had*
*died of the plague a good year ago, the mother and daughter*
*had had to work doubly hard to make ends meet.*

*Sarah, 37, was a herbalist and midwife; Prudence, just*
*16, was a spinner, spinning raw wool on her wheel to create*
*yarn, which she sold to merchants in Cambridge. Prudence*
*had inherited her mother's looks, both having long blonde*
*hair that they tied back beneath linen kerchiefs, vivid green*
*eyes and squat noses, though her mother's furrowed skin*
*spoke of hard days endured.*

*Like the bundles of rosemary, lavender and camomile*
*that hung from the beams of the cottage, their lives were*
*about to become uprooted.*


*"Domp! Domp!" came the knock on the door as Simon*
*Hopkins's staff made heavy contact twice. To Sarah and Pru-*
*dence, it was the sound of doom, which they had been expecting*

since being notified of the witch-finder's arrival the previous evening. Neither woman had slept.

As they stared at one another, frozen, Hopkins's face appeared in the window, and he rapped on the glass with his knuckles. "Open up!" he demanded. "In the name of the Lord!"

In sharp contrast to Henry Drayton's abode, the Sawyers's was tidy and well-kept, a picture of resilience and dignity. A rural scene in cross-stitch and framed floral paintings adorned the walls. The room also smelled rather wonderful: a pervasive bouquet of herbs and wild flowers, the tools of the mother's trade.

A small kitchen area occupied one corner. Next to it were row upon row of variously sized bottles and jars, all neatly labelled: 'Yarrow', 'Feverfew', 'St Johns Wort'… As Hopkins eyed them up, Sarah knew precisely what he was thinking: witches' brews.

She was at her work bench, wearing a simple woollen dress with an apron, preparing a medicinal salve with a pestle and mortar. Prudence, similarly attired, sat at her spinning wheel by the crackling fire. Its gentle whirr-and-clack provided the rhythmic backdrop to their days, but now it had ceased.

"Thou knowest who I am and why the Lord hath sent me," said Hopkins. "The gravest of accusations, of such demonic nature, have been made against thee. Thou art witches."

Sarah threw herself at his feet, clinging to his ankles, while her daughter began to cry. "We aren't witches, sir! I'm a humble herbalist, and my daughter spins her yarn. We never did no harm to that poor woman. Please, sir, you must believe me!"

Kicking, Hopkins freed himself from her grip. "Where be Prickears? And Dainty?"

When both women looked non-plussed, he added: "Thine imps. One a black rabbit, the other a black kitten. Thine demons whom you do suckle."

"Sir," said Sarah, still kneeling on the floor before him, her hands clasped together. "We know nothing of such imps. We are but humble folk who earn a meagre living as herbalist and spinner. We are not witches. If anybody is evil, 'tis that Henry Drayton, making up these tales about us. 'Tis revenge, sir. He..."

"Be quiet, woman!" Hopkins thundered. "The Lord God himself shall judge thee, not I."

He truly believed it.


Hopkins sought out the third alleged witch, Dorothy Kipling, and dragged her from her home. Though her husband protested loudly, he was cowed by the power Hopkins exuded and the threats that he made. She was thrown into the village hall where she tripped and fell. Sarah and Prudence were already there, seated obediently, silently quaking.

When Dorothy looked up, clutching her pained wrist, she noticed two other women from the hamlet: Faith Jarvis and Hester Quill. Jarvis glared at her with folded arms; Quill was *biting her lip, blinking. Both had been hired by Hopkins, to aid his interrogation.*

*Dorothy was an old woman, almost 60, who made jams and preserves with fruit and vegetables from her garden, which she sold at market. Her silver hair was tied in a bun, wisps escaping at the temples. Her grey dress, which had been mended numerous times, was faded and well-worn. She had no teeth.*

## Chapter Fifteen

# Pitchforks at Dawn

Shortly after sunrise on September 5th, 1666, Abby rapped urgently on Jacob's chamber door at The Bull. Before he was even fully awake, she entered.

"We must leave quickly," she told him, throwing open the shutters on his window. "My master's sister is in grave danger."

Jacob swung out of bed and sat up, rubbing his eyes against the daylight, still dressed in his clothes from the night before.

"Mr Standish," she said. "You sleep fully dressed?"

"Mmm. The nights are cold," he mumbled blearily, wishing he were still asleep. In his dream, he had been chasing fleeing figures through a forest of infinitely tall trees, always a few paces behind, and now he would never know the ending.

When he arrived in the tap-room, Abby was polishing off a plate of bread and cheese. Usually, the inn's dog,

Rusty, sat by the table waiting for scraps, but this morning it was nowhere to be seen.

"Finally!" Abby exclaimed, chewing, though he had hardly taken long to compose himself. "We must hurry to Paulina's. According to Hatty, she was set upon by villagers last night."

Thrusting Jacob's cloth-wrapped breakfast into his hand, she was gone.


The inquisitors approached Paulina's home, surprised by how quiet it was, as if nothing had happened. Paulina did not rush from the front door; not a soul was around. Brampton seemed to be the usual rural idyll.

When Jacob rapped on the door, no one answered. He looked through the window and saw Paulina hunched over the dining table, her shoulders juddering in time with her sobs.

Finding the door unlocked, he hastened inside, followed by Abby.

"Mistress Pepys!" he said, his voice choking with concern. "What happened here?"

Paulina lifted her head. Her red eyes were swollen and her flushed cheeks damp. She wore only a long linen chemise, no nightgown, and was shivering. Through cold or fear, they could not tell.

"Oh, Mr Standish!" Paulina wailed, throwing herself at him, too distraught to care about decorum.

Jacob stood woodenly, arms hanging at his sides, wincing. When Abby gently peeled her off, she did not protest.

Returned to her chair, Paulina gradually recovered her spirits sufficiently to relate the night's events.

A good while after the household had retired to bed, Paulina had been awakened by a commotion outside. When she opened her shutters, the scene she beheld churned her insides.

Lit by dancing torchlight were two dozen or so villagers, gathered under her window, some waving pitchforks, others clutching flaming torches. "Their faces were distorted with rage," she said. "They looked like monsters."

"What did they say?" Jacob asked.

Paulina began to weep again, her voice breaking as she spoke. "They called me a witch. They told me I had cursed Goddie Grimston and that his death was on my hands. They began to chant…" Her voice trailed off, overcome by emotion, unable to repeat the words.

Abby had a few ideas, which she did not voice. Most likely, she suspected, they chanted, "Hang the witch!" No innocent woman deserved such terror levelled against her.

"Did you know them?" Abby asked gently.

Paulina gazed up at the inquisitor, her raw eyes pleading. "I knew them all!"

Of course, Brampton was a tight-knit village. One need only witness the rapid circulation of gossip.

Abby rephrased the question: "Who among the mob had made accusations against you?"

She exhaled deeply. "Grimston's sons were there," she recalled barely above a whisper.

"Who was the ringleader?" Jacob asked.

Paulina moaned loudly and buried her head in her arms. "Bulstrode Bennett, sir!"

"He oversteps his authority!" said Jacob. "The actions of a magistrate are to uphold public order, not to incite a mob to terrorise a defenceless woman."

"Aye, but we must tread with caution," Abby warned. "Magistrate Bennett's word is law in Brampton, and he has Lord Fairfax's ear. He's a powerful and dangerous adversary."

Jacob asked Paulina, "What made the mob disperse?"

"My father woke in his chamber, alerted by the chanting. Though he and my mother are both unwell, he ventured outside to challenge them." Her voice faltered. "At length, he persuaded them to disperse. His words still carry some weight in the village."

John Pepys himself appeared in the doorway. He looked even more frail than on the inquisitors' previous visit, his pallid cheeks more sunken, and his breathing in gasps. Abby quickly moved to his side, took him gently by the arm, and guided him to a chair.

After a while, John gathered the strength to take in the candlelit scene. "Young Abigail! And Mr Standish!" he croaked, his recognition dawning. The sight of them clearly cheered his spirits as he managed a sartorial quip: "I see we wear the same shirt, Jacob. You shall become a Pepys yet."

Abby shot Jacob a knowing glance, which he studiously avoided.

The inquisitors were both struck by how a man in such a frail state could have confronted an angry mob on his daughter's behalf. It brought a lump to their throats.

"Father, you must rest," Paulina urged, reaching her hands across the table towards him. "My brother's inquisitors are here now, and they can deal with this terrible matter."

Abby noted with satisfaction that Paulina no longer thought of her as a mere housemaid. She had a burning question on her mind, although she thought twice about asking it. "Forgive me… I know you have been greatly troubled…" she began, then, finding no delicate way to phrase it, simply asked, "Was Will Farlow here on the night of Goddie's death?"

Paulina jolted upright. "Aye, he was here," she replied, adding firmly, "We are to be married at the end of this month, and I love him dearly."

"Did he lay here? In this house?"

Paulina gasped and glanced, horrified, at her father. "Goodness, nay!" she exclaimed. "That would not be…"

Abby's impertinence sparked Paulina's father into life. "I would never countenance such a thing!" he declared, then began coughing violently.

Paulina shook her head miserably and began to cry.

# Chapter Sixteen

# Magistrate & Wife

"What possessed you to ask such a question?" asked a stunned Jacob, when they were safely outside. "Paulina has endured so much, why would you add to her distress?"

"If we're to be diligent inquisitors, Jacob, we must be prepared to ask difficult questions," she replied. "We can't let politics obscure our path to the truth. People will lie to us, and we must discern when they do. Will Farlow claimed he lain with Paulina on the night of Goddie's death, yet she and her father vehemently deny it. If he lied about that, can he be trusted?"

Jacob hesitated. "Then you… You believe Will Farlow killed Goddie? For what reason?"

"I have only theories for now, Jacob, not conclusions."

He was eager to hear them, and she obliged as they pressed onwards, past Rebecca Thacker's front garden.

Paulina Pepys's wedding, she said, had been moved forward after the witchcraft allegations were made. Rebecca had told them so. Whatever fate a witchcraft trial held for Paulina, she seemed determined to face it as a married woman.

They had witnessed first-hand that Farlow was a rogue – a fact to which Paulina seemed blinded. Rebecca had intimated that his interest lay more in the Pepys family name than in Paulina herself. "What if he realised he could retain the Pepys influence, having wed Paulina, then rid himself of his wife?" Abby suggested, to Jacob's great consternation.

Although Goddie's allegations played into his hands, Farlow knew that an accusation of witchcraft might not permanently clear Paulina from his path. However, Goddie's subsequent murder might well serve that purpose, the crime being punishable by death.

"Then Will Farlow murdered Goddie Grimston!" Jacob blurted out.

Embarrassed, he looked around to see whether his outburst had been noticed. But Brampton was quiet. Up ahead, in the grounds of the Church of St Mary Magdalen, the inquisitors saw a handful of people gathered. The church bell began to toll solemnly.

Abby held a finger to her lips. "Please, Jacob, lower your voice. 'Tis only a theory, and it rests on Farlow being a liar. I suspect others may also be playing loose with the truth."

As they drew closer to the activity in the churchyard, they could make out a few faces: a Grimston lad or two, and their mother, Anne. The group was gathered around a plain wooden coffin, their heads bowed. Of course, it was Goddie's funeral, ill-attended as they might have expected.

Hoping they had not been seen, the inquisitors ducked down and ran until they were obscured from the funeral party by the ancient ash trees in the graveyard. Cutting through an area of gravestones, they emerged at the rear of St Mary Magdalen's and joined the main road that traversed the village.

Turning north at a T-junction they soon spied Bulstrode Bennett's house, as Barty Nettlewood had advised they would. It towered above all the thatched, single-storey labourers' cottages around it. Built of red brick, three storeys high, it had been commissioned by a rich London merchant as a countryside retreat.

The innkeeper told them that Bennett, keen to advertise his wealth and prestige, had snapped up the property when the merchant moved abroad. He liked to open his third-floor window and call out to passers-by. Some thought it friendly; most knew he was showing off.

As Abby and Jacob started down the gravel driveway to the house, there came a cry in a voice all too familiar from their nights at The Bull. "Ho there!"

They looked around to see where it was coming from.

"What business have you here?" called out Bulstrode Bennett.

They spotted him, hobbling at a pace towards them from a stable block at the rear of the property. Growing in clumps at the base of the stable wall, Jacob swore he identified more of those deadly black berries.

Two servants were preparing an ornate coach for travel. While one tethered the horses, the other was polishing the black-and-gold paintwork.

"Ho there!" Bennett repeated, furiously waving his arms in the air.

The inquisitors exchanged panicked glances – not that they had expected a gracious welcome.

The magistrate reached them wheezing, his gaunt face flushed puce, though he had stomped only some 30 yards. For someone whose work required an air of sophistication and dignity, his attire, which sagged from his thin frame, was rather… garish.

Ribbons and pearls hung from his breeches and his doublet was dyed a shocking shade of peacock blue. At his chest was an outsized medallion engraved with a family crest, featuring two griffins, a plumed helmet, shield and the scales of justice. (Barty had warned them about the magistrate's ostentatious leanings. Since his family had been successful wool merchants, the primary motif on any family crest really ought to have been a sheep, Barty told them gleefully. Bulstrode, he said, had connived his way to the position of magistrate through political manoeuvring and gratuitous backstabbing.)

"I demand to see your authority to investigate here!" Bennett exclaimed. He squinted in one eye while the other one bulged, making has face seem oddly unbalanced. He looked older than his years and wore an extravagant periwig.

Jacob rose to his full height - considerably higher than Bennett - aware that dealing with pomposity and power was his role in the team. "Sir, we are sent here by Mr Samuel Pepys, Clerk of the Acts to the Navy Board, and acquaintance of King Charles himself."

That seemed to do the trick. Bennett visibly shrank, unaccustomed to being challenged, particularly by employees of acquaintances of royalty. However, his arrogance quickly returned. Brampton was his domain, after all. "Must I repeat myself?" he asked, glowering. "Where is your authority?"

Jacob played for time by looking in his leather bag, though he knew it contained nothing but cheese.

Abby intervened. "Mr Bennett..."

The magistrate silenced her with a stern glare. "Quiet, wench! You shall not address me! I am the magistrate here, and you are a serving girl. Yet you presume to investigate this ungodly act of witchcraft! The only judge in this matter shall be the witch-finder himself, Simon Hopkins, whom I have duly engaged. You two are nought but charlatans."

Jacob attempted to speak: "Mr Pepys…"

Once again, Bennett interjected. "How am I to be sure that you are indeed here on behalf of this Mr Pepys, when you present to me no letter of authority? For all I am aware, you have concocted the gentleman from thin air." Bennett sneered, enjoying himself.

Pepys had told the inquisitors that he was acquainted with the magistrate - had referred to him as "an indecent fool" - so it seemed certain that Bennett was lying. But what could they do?

Preening a dangling pearl, the magistrate continued, "As a matter of fact, I ride to Huntingdon forthwith, to secure from Sir Edward Mallory a Letter of Marque, authorising me to detain those I deem to be obstructing justice." He smiled slickly. "If you do not leave Brampton by sunset tomorrow, I shall have you jailed."

With that, he turned on his expensive heel and returned to his waiting carriage.

"He's very keen to see us gone," Abby noted drily.

Jacob could not accept his threat as calmly. "What shall we do?" he asked through gritted teeth. "Mr Pepys will never forgive me. And what of his sister?"

"What we shall do, Mr Standish, is to speak with Helen Bennett."

Jacob performed a double-take. "Speak? With the magistrate's wife? But that would only enrage him further!"

"Precisely," said Abigail, grinning broadly.

Jacob's expression darkened. "Then I fear we are playing with fire."

A servant showed the inquisitors into a grand, high-ceilinged drawing room, as ostentatious as her husband's garb: a finely engraved harpsichord, gilt mirrors, floor-to-ceiling crimson drapes, and intricate frescoes depicting gods, angels and... indeed there he was: Bulstrode Bennett himself, astride a winged unicorn. The furniture was all rich, upholstered oak. Logs blazed in an enormous fireplace.

Helen Bennett, in her early fifties, was seated in a gilt armchair so ornate it could have doubled as a throne. A male servant was fanning her with an exotic feather, while a female servant primped her extravagantly coiffed hair. On noticing Abby and Jacob, she dismissed both servants, who bowed, curtsied, and departed the room like wraiths.

"I thought my husband would have frightened you off," she said, regarding them over her nose.

Jacob bowed and began stammering an apology, which she silenced with a dismissive gesture.

"Good for you," she said. "The man's a bully and a lout."

Abby couldn't help smirking; Jacob merely looked bewildered.

"Come," she said, pointing to a footstool. "Be seated."

The inquisitors regarded the stool with puzzlement; they would not both fit on there.

"I am content to stand," Jacob said loftily, offering Abby the stool.

Both had noticed a distinctive pungency - a scent of sandalwood and mint - the moment they entered the room. A perfume, so liberally applied, it overpowered the aromas of the burning wood in the fireplace and the leather of the furniture.

"Mistress Bennett," said Jacob. "I cannot help but notice…"

"The elegance of the decor?" she second-guessed him. "The style is all mine, I assure you."

Jacob adjusted his periwig. "Your taste is indeed exquisite, Mistress Bennett, however I was referring to your perfume, which is… equally exquisite."

"It is Bulstrode's favourite," she told him. "I wear it solely because it is the only one he chooses to purchase. Unfortunately, my husband has the good taste of a farmyard sow."

Reading the room, Abby took a gamble. "Mistress Bennett, it appears that you and your husband don't…"

"Like one another?" she interjected. "Nay, we do not! Cheeky young wench."

Abby lowered her head. "I assure you that was not…"

Waving such frippery aside, Helen lifted a necklace from her throat. It glittered and sparkled as she did so. "I would ask you: how many diamonds and sapphires do you own?"

"None," Jacob replied dutifully.

Helen tutted. "I was aware of that, you silly fellow. My point is this: What are you prepared to endure in exchange for extravagance and luxury? Our days are numbered, after all. Such is God's way. For certain gentleman, we pray, the count may be mercifully brief."

Jacob was dumbstruck. Was she wishing her husband… dead?

Abby shifted uncomfortably on the small footstool. "Mistress Bennett, may I ask…?"

"You may not."

"…What you make of this talk of witchcraft and the death of Goddie Grimston?"

"Oh!" shrieked the old woman, fanning herself as if about to faint. "Do not mention that vile pickthank's name in this house! Besmirching the reputation of a lady! Good riddance to the foul knave, I say."

Jacob's voice finally returned. "A foul knave besmirched your reputation?"

"Cease this insolent chatter!" Helen exclaimed. "I will not hear his name in this house!" She rose, theatrically swooning as she staggered around the room, all the while shrieking for her servant. "Benjamin! Benjamin!" When Benjamin appeared, she ordered him, "Show the visitors out! They bring nought but pestilent air! I shall have to lie down!"

# Chapter Seventeen

# A New Curse

Abby and Jacob headed back in the direction of the church, with plans to refresh themselves at The Bull. They felt certain, or at least dearly hoped, that Goddie's funeral had finished by now.

"We must discover in what manner Goddie Grimston wronged Helen Bennett," Abby said.

"Aye," Jacob replied, "I…" A hacking cough stopped him in his tracks.

Abby patted his back. "You look drawn, Jacob," she said, when he had recovered. "Perhaps we should rest this afternoon? We've worked hard and accomplished a great deal in such a short time."

He would hear none of it. "Nonsense! Simon Hopkins may arrive in Brampton at any moment. We must clear Paulina's name in all haste."

Just then, a distant woman's voice could be heard calling out urgently, "Mr Standish!"

Up ahead, they saw Paulina Pepys emerge from the churchyard and run towards them. Her face looked drawn with concern.

Breathlessly, Paulina related how two nights ago, Rebecca Thacker had stormed into her house demanding to speak with her father. An argument had ensued, concerning an alleged overcharge for clothing he had commissioned. Paulina had no idea where the innuendo had originated, she told them (and Jacob wisely did not tell her).

Her friend had spoken harshly to her father, culminating in her wishing a pox on him and his family. "She was in a rage and did not truly mean it," Paulina said.

She went on, struggling to maintain composure, "This morning, after you departed, my father became gravely ill. I helped him undress and put him to bed. My mother had not risen since the terrible events of last night. Despite all my attempts with herbal remedies, nothing has cured them.

"My father is stubborn and refuses to see a physician. I fear gravely for his life… It left me no choice. I sought out Archibald Bramwell and implored him to visit, against my father's wishes." With that, she broke down into sobs.

Abby found herself becoming irritated by her master's sister's propensity for tears. She had learned that it paid to be resilient.

At length, Paulina was able to continue. "The physician spoke with my mother, and the argument with Rebecca was mentioned. My mother began repeating that she was cursed by a witch, insisting that Rebecca's witchcraft had confined them to their beds and blighted their souls."

"Have your parents not been ill for some time?" asked Jacob.

"Aye," Paulina replied, "though it was only today they were confined to their beds."

"Perhaps your mother attributed the witchcraft to Rebecca, in the hope it might divert the same charge from you?" Abby suggested, wondering whether family loyalty might explain the outburst.

"Nay!" wailed Paulina. "They are friends! My mother was suffering from delirium! She did not know what she was saying!"

Jacob put a comforting hand on Paulina's shoulder, which calmed her. "Then we must ensure that word of this does not spread further," he said.

Paulina's head dropped. "We are too late, Mr Standish. Being employed by the Ravenscourt estate, Bramwell told me he was obliged to report any accusation of witchcraft to the local magistrate."

"Bulstrode Bennett!" the inquisitors exclaimed in unison.

The three of them returned to the Pepys home. They came up with a plan, and Paulina began to brighten.

They would leave John and Margaret in the care of a trusted friend – not Rebecca Thacker, for obvious reasons – and would walk together into Huntingdon. There, they would seek out Sir Edward Mallory, whom Bennett had mentioned as a senior legal figure, to appeal to him for sense and reason.

If Bennett's superior did not harbour the same fervent belief in witchcraft, they hoped he might be a powerful ally. (Actually, Abby, who was familiar with the political wheedlings of her master's friends in high places, was sceptical. She believed such men were easily swayed by popular opinion to protect their power. But she did not let on.)

As they left the Pepys's house, Jacob checked around the foot of the door. "No poppet," he pointed out. "Yet they claim Rebecca's witchcraft is at play."

# Chapter Eighteen

# Hopkins Interrogates

*T*he tests for witchcraft were simple and effective, as practised by Simon's father on countless occasions. The first one involved searching the accused women's bodies for witches' marks: often resembling teets, although any discolouration or blemish might arouse suspicion. It was through these that witches were said to suckle their demonic familiars, having first made a covenant with the Devil himself, to serve him, denying God and Jesus Christ.

The Witchcraft Act of 1541 was the first to set out penalties, including execution and the forfeiture of possessions, for those practising witchcraft. It was enacted during the reign of Henry VIII, and forbade anyone to:

"...use, devise, practise or exercise, or cause to be devised, practised or exercised, any invocations or conjurations of Sprites, witchcrafts, enchantments or sorceries with the intent of finding money or treasure, or to waste, consume or destroy

*any person, or to provoke any person to unlawful love, or for*
*any other unlawful intent or purpose…"*

It was repealed six years later but brought back under
Elizabeth I as the Witchcraft Act Against Conjurations, Enchantments and Witchcrafts of 1562. This had then been
broadened under James I, in 1603, removing a small hope
once afforded accused clergymen, that they would be tried
by a more lenient ecclesiastical court. (Although witches were
predominantly female, around one-tenth of those executed for
the crime were men.)

It was this 1603 Witchcraft Act against Conjuration,
Witchcraft and Dealing with Evil and Wicked Spirits that
empowered Matthew Hopkins, and later his son.

*So he reacted with fury when Faith Jarvis and Hester Quill*
*sought him out at The Blacksmith's Inn, to tell him in faltering*
*voices that they had found no suspicious marks on any of the*
*three accused witches' bodies.*

*Jarvis offered, "There was a mark on Sarah Sawyer, in the*
*region of…"*

*But Quill cut her off. "That was a mole, sir. I'd swear to it."*

*"The Devil himself works with these witches to conceal their*
*wickedness!" Hopkins thundered, launching his hat against a*
*wall. Then, calming, he beckoned the women closer and spoke*
*in a conspiratorial tone: "But they shall not escape justice, for*
*God is on our side. We shall watch them together on this night.*

*And the next night. And the next, as it may be so necessary.*
*We shall witness the witches conjure their imps, and then*
*they shall confess."*

*So began the second test: watching. It was a laborious*
*process, waiting for the accused women to summon their*
*familiars, which would prove them to be witches. Such was*
*Hopkins's conviction, he felt assured of success.*

*Yet no imps came.*

*Faith Jarvis nodded off first, seated in the village hall*
*around midnight, while Hopkins paced the room distracted-*
*ly. When the accused old woman, Dorothy Kipling's head*
*fell to her chest, he lunged towards the poor wretch and*
*shook her chair violently.*

*"Nay, witch! You shall not sleep!" he told her.*

*"Sir," she pleaded through withered gums. "Why do you*
*strike me? I am but an old woman who hash done no evil."*

*"Thou art a witch!" he railed. "Conjure thine imp, the*
*demon Pluck, and we may be done."*

*She shook her head pitifully. "I have no imp, shir."*

*This went on, as Hopkins had considered it might, for*
*three days and three nights. Jarvis and Quill rested in*
*shifts while Hopkins, powered by righteous fervour, barely*
*slept, catching an hour here or there, and commanding his*
*watchers not to allow a witch to do the same.*

*The accused women were walked around the room, shuffling in a trance-like state, as if they were sleepwalking. Quill one time spoke up for them, asking for mercy on their behalf, but Hopkins only threatened to dock her pay, and she fell silent.*

*Dorothy Kipling, along with Prudence and Sarah Sawyer, grew pale, scarlet-eyed and feverish, and cried out, begging to be freed, or protesting their innocence. At one point, Prudence began laughing hysterically and was hushed angrily by the witch-finder. Still no imps came.*

*On the third night, Hopkins switched to a new tactic: he would take each woman alone into a back room and interrogate her one-on-one. Faith Jarvis would accompany him as a witness and take notes (since Hester Quill was unable to read or write).*

*It was then that he made his breakthrough.*


*As he returned to the hall, Prudence Sawyer shuffled behind him, head bowed, ghostly white. Her mother looked up blankly. Dorothy Kipling had fallen asleep.*

*Hopkins, who now resembled something conjured by demons himself, planted his leather boots apart and slammed his staff into the floor, waking Kipling with a start.*

*"The girl hath confessed to witchcraft!" he announced.*

*Quill gasped. Sarah Sawyer and Dorothy Kipling did not register. Their minds were filled with anguished voices, and their eyes registered only a blur.*

*Paying off his two watchers - three shillings apiece - Hopkins locked the condemned women in the hall for the rest of the night and finally, blessedly, they were allowed to sleep.*

*Prudence had confessed to him that she had cursed Henry Drayton's wife, Lucy. That she had sent her familiar, Dainty, to poison the woman's milk, which had been denied to her mother. And that when Lucy died, they had greatly rejoiced and held a sabbat, attended by their imps, Prickears, Dainty and Pluck.*

*Hopkins was assiduous in his work. He was only too aware that many had escaped justice and God's retribution through a lack of evidence, or by questioning the methods through which that evidence had been obtained. He would dot every i and cross every t. None would slip through his net.*

*"You were aided in this witchcraft by Dorothy Kipling?" he asked Prudence.*

*"Aye," she replied.*

*"And by your mother, Sarah Sawyer?"*

*"Aye," she replied.*

*With that word, poor Prudence may have condemned her own mother, whom she loved with all her heart, to death.*

# Chapter Nineteen

# To Huntingdon

Paulina hesitated to leave her parents, even under the care of her good friend, Mabel Fenwick. As an experienced midwife, Mabel was well-versed in healthcare, yet Paulina feared her parents were so gravely ill that they might not survive even her brief absence.

Sensing this, Mabel reassured her. "The walk will do you good," she said. "T'ain't healthy to be cooped up indoors all day, tending to the sick. John and Margaret will be fine with me, don't 'e worry."

The mood remained sombre as they crossed Nun's Bridge and joined George Street, with Fairfax's estate sprawling to their left. Far ahead, they could make out a horse and rider heading also towards Huntingdon.

It was mid-morning, and the weather was kind: a cloudless sky and a comforting sun once again. To the inquisitors, Huntingdonshire was an oasis of vitality, and around every bend was a new vista of lush, verdant wonderment.

To Paulina, it was a prison, albeit a pleasant one; she missed the city and its culture. She too had grown up in London, the tenth of John and Margaret's eleven children. In fact, she was the Pepys's second daughter named Paulina; her tragic younger namesake had only lived to the age of four, so they had never been acquainted.

Hers was a life of servitude. When her elder brother, Samuel, invited her to live with him and his wife, Elizabeth, at Seething Lane, it was not as a guest but as his wife's maid. He had even accused her of stealing scissors from Elizabeth and a book from his own maid. She was not allowed to dine with them, and Samuel soon made it clear that he had grown tired of her presence.

When the Brampton cottage became available, she was sent there to care for their elderly parents in situ. It was not what she had had in mind for her future.

More than anything, she longed for a husband who would free her from this dreary life, grant her independence, and love her for who she truly was. Samuel had meddled in her affairs far too often, suggesting ill-matched suitors. Among them, she recalled the upholsterer Philip Harman and Benjamin Gauden, son of a Navy victualler, both from London. Neither had proved suitable.

Only last March, Samuel and her father had paired her with the Brampton landowner, Robert Endsum, whom she had found to be an ill-bred drunkard, uncultured in his ways. When she had told Samuel so, it had only encouraged his pursuit of the arrangement! Thankfully, Endsum had passed away.

Paulina resented her brother's overbearing manner and he, her truculence. He appeared to think as lowly of her as she did highly of herself.

"Do you like it here in Brampton?" Abby asked Paulina, stopping briefly to pet a grazing cow.

"Very much so," Paulina replied, before returning to her introspection.


As they walked, the inquisitors chatted, and Abby imparted some of the local history she had learned from her master. Oliver Cromwell, who ruled England with religious fervour until 1658, was born in Huntingdon, she explained. He had gathered troops there to join his New Model Army and fight as parliamentarians against the royalist forces of King Charles I.

Cromwell's iron fist was still fresh in both their minds, even though they were mere children during that turbulent period. Every English citizen's life had been affected by the self-proclaimed Lord Protector, no place more so than London, where soldiers roamed the streets and rules were strictly enforced.

As a Puritan, they were well aware, Cromwell believed that life should be lived with purity, according to the writings of the Bible. Entertainment devoid of piety had been frowned upon. Inns and theatres were closed down, and many sports were banned (although Oliver himself managed to enjoy a game of bowling... and to father an illegitimate child).

Sunday became a day of church, rest and religious contemplation; Jacob remembered being chased by soldiers for the 'crime' of playing football. Profanity was punishable by a fine, while repeated profanity necessitated a custodial sentence. Make-up was banned, and they had seen soldiers scrubbing women's faces in the street. Clothing in general became plain and muted.

Christmas, which had developed into a day of joyful feasting, was returned to its religious significance: a celebration of the birth of Jesus Christ. Decorations were banned, and soldiers entered houses from which the aroma of roasting goose emanated, to confiscate the food.

Master Pepys had admitted to Abby that he had been a strong advocate of the republic under the Lord Protector, and that when his successor, Charles II, came to the throne in 1660, he had switched his allegiance to the monarchy. Her Master Pepys was adept at supporting a winner, she was well aware.

Agricultural fields backed by rows of houses greeted the trio's arrival in Huntingdon. They passed a large enclosed bowling field. Abby had to dissuade an over-excited Jacob from dropping by for a game, reminding him of their duty to her master.

He began to admonish himself, but his voice crackled, and he began to choke. His cough had been worsening, Abby had noticed, and told him so. He brushed her concerns aside.

George Street took them into the heart of the town, past the George Inn and All Saints' Church, towards the market square off the high street. Paulina knew her brother had attended the Free Grammar School -an education denied to her - and that Oliver Cromwell had studied there before him.

"Where shall we go?" asked Jacob, taking in the busy market, where vendors were hawking their wares and children darted about. A street musician could be heard playing the popular tune of the day, Flow My Tears, on a lute, and singing…

*Flow, my tears, fall from your springs!*
*Exiled for ever, let me mourn;*
*Where night's black bird her sad infamy sings,*
*There let me live forlorn.*

Paulina and the inquisitors agreed to ask after Sir Edward Mallory's place of work at an inn, where they would take dinner. The life of an inquisitor, Abby and

Jacob were coming to realise, often involved appeasing an empty stomach.

So they retraced their steps to the George, a large coaching inn with a courtyard, which they entered via a timber-bolstered walkway. Before them, an external staircase led up and around the upper tier of guest rooms.

Upon entering the tap-room, they were as shocked to see Anne Grimston as she was to see them. The unexpected encounter diverted their attention, so the usually eagle-eyed Jacob did not notice Will Farlow exit hastily through a back door, leaving a perplexed young woman at his table.

"My!" Anne exclaimed, rising. A shaft of sunlight illuminated her tankard. "'Tis you pair! And young mistress Pepys! What brings you to these parts?"

They exchanged tales. Anne, for her part, was dealing with the sorry aftermath of her husband's death. Although Goddie had been a successful farmer, enough to purchase his own fields, he had been a useless husband and father, she told them. "Clod drank all our money."

The parish priest, who had conducted Goddie's funeral service only that morning, had advised her to see a man of law as soon as possible, to discuss her "dower rights". She had never heard of such a thing, she said, and the solicitor she had just visited to discuss these "dower rights" had only confused her further.

Anne opened her bag, allowing them a glimpse of thick paperwork. "Made my poor head twirl," she told them, mimicking a twirling motion with her hand.

"Your husband did not leave a Will?" Jacob asked.

"Leave a Will?" Anne shrieked. "All he left me was his cold, dead body. And that's now buried." She crossed herself. "Lord have mercy upon his worthless soul."

They were glad when she left, since none relished Anne Grimston's incessant chatter. Jacob ordered an eel pie, and its nourishment lifted their spirits. Paulina kept glancing at him, then averting her eyes, he noticed. He wondered whether she had something on her mind.

Abby asked Paulina about Helen Bennett and the grave injustice Goddie Grimston had done to her.

"The whole village knows," Paulina replied, picking an eel bone from between her teeth.

*Naturally!* thought the inquisitors.

Every autumn, Paulina explained, the Brampton Harvest Fair was held on the village green. Music, dance, craft and food stalls, sack races, archery... A celebration of village life and of a bountiful harvest.

An artist from Huntingdon had hired a stall, displaying his paintings of local landscapes; he had also offered for sale sketches of people who would sit for him. One who had done so, Paulina recalled, was Helen Bennett. When the artwork was finished and Helen was admiring it, Goddie Grimston appeared, skipping drunkenly.

"Goddie drew his own caricature of Helen, and waved it under her nose," Paulina told the inquisitors. "She hated it! He made her look like a toad. Her shrieking gathered a crowd, which only made her worse. Then Bulstrode appeared and dragged Goddie away by his collar. She took an age to calm, ranting about taking Goddie to court, to clear her good name.

"Nought came of her threats. Can you imagine Goddie's caricature being held up in a court of law as evidence?" Paulina giggled, her laughter a rare bright moment during these trying times for the Pepyses of Brampton.

When the table fell silent, Paulina held Jacob's gaze and said quietly, "There is something else…"

He put a hand on her arm. "Pray tell, dear lady. You must know that any secret is safe with us."

Abby nodded.

Paulina blinked and looked down. "I lied to you in front of my father. I did have congress with Will Farlow on the night of Goddie's death."

Jacob slapped the table in frustration, while Abby remained composed.

"I dared not admit… with my father present…" Paulina stumbled over her words. "He would have…" She trailed off.

Jacob asked, "How did he enter your chamber without your father's knowledge?"

"I leave a ladder for him, and my window open. My parents' hearing ails, and they are sorely weakened these days. Will departs before the sun rises."

Jacob pursed his lips. *Just because Will Farlow told one awkward truth, it does not make him trustworthy,* he mused.

Abby took out her suspect list and crossed out Farlow's name.

The George's innkeeper knew of Sir Edward Mallory and directed them to the Senior Magistrate's office in the Town Hall.

They found the stone building on the market square. Inside, the hall was flooded with light, its floor paved with flagstones worn smooth by so many feet. Wooden beams supported the roof, and an unoccupied platform at the far end, laid out with high-backed chairs and a table, looked set for public proceedings.

The space was busy with people - clerks, lawyers, merchants, members of the public - milling about, and Jacob pushed through them, followed by Abby and Paulina, in search of Sir Edward's office. Voices echoed, combining to create a sense of importance.

Among the rooms lined around the hall, Jacob finally came upon one with this sign on its door:

## Sir Edward Mallory
## Senior Magistrate for the County of Hunting-donshire

Abby wished her master were with them. Here was a powerful man she would find intimidating.

Inside, a clerk listened to Jacob's nervily related tale, then bade them wait while he consulted with Sir Edward, and disappeared into an adjoining office.

Jacob's eyes darted around the room, taking in its rows of legal volumes, framed official documents and notices of local governance. "Will you speak with Sir Edward?" he asked Abby.

"Nay!" she hissed back. "How can I…"

A door creaked open, and Abby fell silent. The trio waited stiffly for the clerk to reach them.

"Sir Edward has graciously consented to meet with you," he said. "I request that you be mindful of that, and detain him only briefly."

Abby noticed that Jacob's hands were shaking.

Sir Edward Mallory's office walls were covered with imposing, gilt-framed portraits of men in robes and wigs. One clearly depicted Sir Edward himself, his gaze stern and commanding. The others, his predecessors no doubt, were no less unnerving. Their eyes seemed to bore into the visitors, silently judging their presence.

The gentleman himself was seated upright behind a desk neatly stacked with papers. He wore a dark robe, a silk cravat, a curly grey periwig, and a gold signet ring on one finger. There was a lengthy scar across his forehead, which greatly perturbed Jacob, who suspected it was a memento of the Civil War.

Mallory's presence reminded Jacob all too vividly of his headmaster's, in whose study he had been soundly beaten on so many occasions. Unnerved, he removed not just his hat, but also his periwig, and wrung them in his hands. When the Senior Magistrate stared at him as if he were mad, he noticed the error and slapped them both back onto his head, where they remained, skewed, for the duration of the meeting.

Matters were off to a poor start.

Jacob managed to introduce the three of them and stammered out the reason for their presence. Mr Samuel Pepys's inquisitors; Goddie Grimston's allegations of witchery; Rebecca and Paulina's innocence...

Mallory stopped him and addressed Paulina. "Are you a witch?" he asked bluntly.

Paulina's mouth wordlessly opened and closed.

Jacob had no choice but to speak on her behalf. "Nay, she is no witch, your honour. I can..."

Mallory glared at him. "Let the woman speak for herself!" he thundered.

It shocked Paulina into action. "I am no witch, sir," she confirmed timidly.

"Your honour," Jacob piped up, "Mr Bennett…"

"*I am aware of Mr Bennett's involvement, Mr Standish!*" Mallory bellowed. "My esteemed Brampton colleague wishes for your incarceration. He visited me this morning, and I did sign for him a Letter of Marque. It grants Bennett the power to arrest you."

Paulina gasped. The inquisitors blinked incredulously.

Sir Edward continued, "You have no authority here, yet you act like agents of the Crown itself. Let it be known that such behaviour is neither condoned nor welcomed in this jurisdiction."

"Your honour, we act on behalf of Mr Samuel Pepys, whose sister stands beside me," Jacob protested meekly. "He is Clerk of the Acts to the…"

"I know who Mr Pepys is!" Mallory thundered. "He a friend of the Lord Fairfax himself. My point is that you possess no formal proof of your association with him!"

Jacob's cough returned suddenly, and he bent over, struggling for breath.

Mallory leaned over his desk, addressing Jacob directly. "Mr Standish, do you bring illness into my office?"

"Nay, sir!" Jacob assured him between fits of choking. "It is a cold. Nought else."

Finally, Abby found her nerve. "Your honour, I beg you, a grave miscarriage of justice is taking place. Simon Hopkins rides…"

Again, Sir Edward interrupted, preferring the sound of his own voice. "Simon Hopkins brings with him public scrutiny. In this matter, I am obliged to adhere strictly to the letter of the law."

*Is he offering us a glimmer of hope?* Abby wondered. "Sir, are you saying you may be able to intervene, if Hopkins transgresses the law in his methods?"

Adjusting his cravat, Mallory ignored her question. "In order for you to continue your investigation, and to avoid incarceration, I would require a Special Commission of Inquiry, duly authorised by the Admiralty."

Abby, despite herself, persisted. "As to Simon Hopkins's methods, your honour?"

"If he does transgress the law, I may be able to intervene. Now, I insist that you leave. You have taken up enough of my time already."

# Hopkins Challenged

*S*imon Hopkins did not have to seek out a Cambridge magistrate. A Cambridge magistrate came to him, having been summoned by Dorothy Kipling's frantic husband, Walter. He woke Hopkins at The Blacksmith's Inn in the early hours of the morning following Prudence Sawyer's confession.

Having slept for barely eight hours in the last 72, the self-appointed witch-finder was groggy as the door to his chamber was flung open by a man whose face he recognised but could not immediately place.

Gradually, his mists cleared. "Mr... Langton? Mr Edward Langton?" Hopkins asked, focusing with one bleary eye.

Both men had attended Cambridge University together, though Langton had been finishing postgraduate studies in law as Hopkins entered its hallowed arches.

They might never have been acquainted, had Langton not been handed a pamphlet Hopkins had printed, criticising the Church of England for its retention of elements of Catholicism, demanding they be reformed. Langton, a moderate Protestant, had taken umbrage. Heated words were exchanged, and the pamphlets were gathered up and destroyed.

Moreover, Langton's father was Sir William Langton, an influential member of parliament, known for his philanthropic endeavours and initiatives to help the poor and needy, in particular the Langton Almshouses.

It did not bode well.

"Simon Hopkins!" Langton replied cheerily. "Did I ever consider that we might meet again? And in circumstances of such intrigue!"

Hopkins sat upright on his straw mattress and rubbed his sallow cheeks.

Langton looked as imposing as ever. He removed his hat, revealing side-parted dark hair. His features were chiselled and he was clean-shaven.

His clothing was immaculate, if understated: a navy-blue doublet with fine brass buttons and matching breeches, polished leather boots, and a dark velvet cloak. The white ruff around his neck marked him as part of the judiciary, and Hopkins quickly snapped to attention.

"Sir, you are…?" he began.

"A magistrate, Mr Hopkins. Indeed. A Justice of the Peace. That is why I am here. For I hear the peace has been mightily shattered in this fine hamlet. By you, Mr Hopkins."

"*My methods, sir, were laid down by King James himself, in the name of God and Jesus Christ. I would defend them with my last breath.*"

"*Then we must hope it does not come to that. Must we not?*"

*A chill descended that afternoon. The village hall was cold, such that steam rose off the crowds packed in to watch the interrogation of Simon Hopkins. How the tables had turned.*

*The Blacksmith's Inn's landlord was there with his wife. As were Henry Drayton, whose wife, Lucy, had perished, and Hopkins's watchers, Faith Jarvis and Hester Quill. Walter Kipling, Dorothy's aged husband, stood at the front of the crowd, a gentle hand on his wife's shoulder.*

*The three accused women - Sarah and Prudence Sawyer, and Dorothy Kipling - sat centre-stage, their ashen, clammy skin a reminder of the nightmare they had endured, though each had changed into fresh woollens, neatly pressed and dignified.*

*The Cambridge magistrate, Edward Langton, sat at the back of the hall on a hastily constructed platform, sporting a fine periwig. He had spent the morning speaking with the accused women and other witnesses, including the physician who had attempted to treat the victim, Lucy Drayton.*

*Simon Hopkins stood before him in his father's outfit, now much rumpled, pleading his case.*

"*Sir, I hold in my hand the confessions of these witches,*" *said Hopkins. "May I present them to thee?*"

"Mr Hopkins, I am aware of these confessions of which you speak. Were they not acquired under duress?"

The crowd cried out and jeered. Langton hushed them.

Hopkins spoke again: "Nay, sir, they…"

A renewed commotion interrupted him, and the magistrate warned the villagers that they must calm their emotions and let the man speak.

Someone called out, "He is not a man. He is the Devil himself!" When several cheered, others glared at them.

Hopkins looked fit to burst. "I am God's messenger on earth, sir! I would rid this place of evil! They," he pointed with his staff at the Sawyers and Kipling, "be the devils!"

Sarah Sawyer looked up and fixed his gaze. "Nay, sir, I am no devil. Nor is my daughter, who you treated with such malice."

"Nor my wife!" shouted Walter Kipling, when Dorothy failed to speak up, to murmurs of assent.

"Is it not true," began the magistrate, Langton, "that you did deny these poor women sleep, for three days and nights?"

"It is not, sir," Hopkins lied.

All hell broke loose.

When it was finally quelled, Hopkins spoke. "Whose word wouldst thou believe, sir? That of peasants? Or of the Witch-finder General himself?" It was the first time he had referred to himself using his father's erstwhile title. He puffed himself up and stared down the magistrate.

Sarah Sawyer spoke. "'Tis true, your honour, that he made us sit in this very hall for three days and three nights, and that when we tried to sleep, he woke us and made us walk about."

"She lies!" Hopkins declared. "For she be a witch!"

The witch-finder shook his head, smiling, as the catcalls rang out. He had them. It was his word, an educated man's, against theirs.

Amid all the noise, Hester Quill tentatively raised her hand. As people noticed her, they ceased their ranting, until absolute silence remained.

Langton looked quizzically at the plainly dressed woman with the weathered face.

She spoke in a quiet, faltering voice. "Your honour, I was there also. Mr Hopkins," she did not dare look him in the eye, "employed me as a watcher, sir. It is true that he denied these women sleep for three days and nights, just as you said."

You could have heard a quill drop.

"An independent witness," proclaimed Langton. "What say you, Simon Hopkins?"

But Hopkins wasn't finished. "I pray thee call the physician who did examine these witches' unfortunate victim, sir. For his testimony will surely be damning."

A gentleman pushed forward through the crowd while everyone stared, transfixed by the proceedings. He stood out for the quality of his clothing and for his obvious attention to hygiene.

"*Jasper Milton, physician,*" *he announced when he was standing before Langton. "At your service.*"

*It was the first time the witch-finder had set eyes on the man, and he realised he should have questioned the physician himself. In its place, he offered up a prayer to the Almighty.*

"*You did examine the unfortunate victim in this matter - one Lucy Drayton - sir?*" *asked the magistrate.*

"*I did, sir,*" *said Milton.*

"*And what is your professional opinion, concerning the sickness of said victim?*"

*Henry Drayton shook his fists, shouting: "My wife was cursed by these witches!*"

"*Be silent, Mr Drayton!*" *roared Langton. "Pray continue, Dr Milton.*"

"*Sir, Lucy Drayton was afflicted with a fever that worsened over several days. Besides my administrations of rosemary and sage, I employed leeches for bloodletting. I also purged her with jalap root, in the hope of expelling the malady. Alas, my endeavours were fruitless, and she died on the seventh day of her illness.*"

"*Was any mark present on the body of Lucy Drayton?*"

"*There was, sir.*"

*Hopkins's dark eyes lit up. "By way of the witches' curse!*"

*The physician shook his head. "On the contrary, sir. It was a mark I have witnessed on many unfortunates in my practice. It was a bubo, sir.*"

"Then your professional opinion, Mr Milton," said Langton, "is that Lucy Drayton did succumb to the bubonic plague?"

"It is, sir."

The witch-finder had one final, desperate trick up his sleeve. Or in his pocket, as it turned out.

Hopkins produced what looked like a very thin dagger: an iron needle about six inches long, set into a wooden handle. It was a witch-pricking needle.

He addressed the magistrate. "Sir, I stand by these confessions. With thy permission, I would prick these women. If they do not bleed, then surely they are witches."

Langton had heard of this practice of pricking. While it was derided by men of science, he was loathe to deny Hopkins's request so publicly.

"Very well," he said.

Hopkins himself entirely trusted the process.

Each woman in turn exposed her back, and the witch-finder gently pressed the needle into their flesh, praying under his breath that no blood would appear.

First, Dorothy Kipling. A red drop of blood instantly appeared, to great cheers.

Next, Sarah Sawyer. The same.

Finally, young Prudence Sawyer. The one who had confessed. As Hopkins pricked her then stood back, peering intently, no blood came. The spectators collectively inhaled.

*"Witness the witch!" Hopkins cried out, just as a tiny red speck appeared at the point where he had pricked the girl, which grew into a perfect crimson sphere, then fell, weaving a fine, bloody trail down her back.*

*For years afterwards, many present would recount the spectacle of the trial with grim satisfaction.*

*Henry Drayton was discovered to have held lingering grudges, for petty reasons – an enclosure gate not properly shut; a perceived slight concerning his ability to hold ale – against the Sawyers and Kipling. He was fined and forced to publicly apologise.*

*Simon Hopkins's public humiliation was deemed sufficient punishment; given that no lasting harm had been done to any person, Edward Langton allowed him to go free. Perhaps the old Cambridge association had softened the magistrate's judgment – although Hopkins was warned of dire consequences, should he not cease his witch-finding practice.*

*The chastened Puritan departed on horseback as he had arrived, jeered by a crowd and followed by young boys who threw stones at him.*

*Never again would he endure such humiliation, he vowed. He had been foolish to begin his work in a place where he had not known the local magistrate, that he might cajole him towards his way of thinking.*

*In Brampton, he assured himself, events would turn out very differently. The magistrate there, Bulstrode Bennett, had actively sought him out. He had ridden from Huntingdonshire to Essex to seek his counsel and to request his services. They were men of the same mind: that witches must be tried and punished, by means of the old methods.*

*To balance matters in his favour, he planned to return to Cambridge to seek out a godly carpenter.*

# Chapter Twenty-One

# A Door Slams Shut

Outside Huntingdon Town Hall, Jacob became animated; even Paulina forced a smile.

"If Simon Hopkins breaks the law, then we have him!" he exclaimed excitedly, seeking affirmation in Abby's expression but finding none.

But instead, she looked fretful. "Simon Hopkins will operate just as his father did. He will deny everything and hide his methods from scrutiny. He won't be caught breaking the law. Matthew Hopkins was cunning, and I expect nothing less from his wicked son."

She went on urgently, "Worse, we've learned that Bulstrode Bennett reached Sir Edward before us and now holds legal authority to have Jacob and I thrown in jail. We can be certain he will use it. 'Tis essential we contact my master immediately concerning the Special Commission of Inquiry Sir Edward mentioned."

Jacob, who enjoyed being spurred into action, nodded decisively. "Then I shall seek out a post-house and dispatch a messenger forthwith, offering him a handsome sum to ensure he accepts my charge. He shall ride to London through the night."

The sun was hovering above the horizon, like a benign, watchful eye over the landscape, as the inquisitors and Paulina reached her parents' home. Paulina raised her eyes skyward and clasped her hands together, offering up a prayer, before opening the door and rushing upstairs. Abby and Jacob followed.

The first chamber on the landing was John Pepys's and they found Paulina inside, holding the old man's hand. Mabel Fenwick was sitting beside the bed, sewing. The space smelled of herbs - lavender for relaxation, chamomile against fever - that had been placed on the windowsills and nestled on John's pillow. On the dresser, an array of jars containing variously coloured herbal tinctures and syrups were lined up, some with their lids off - remedies already tried.

They were heartened to find old John sitting up, though he remained pale and weak, his chest rattling with each breath. As usual, he found strength to greet his son's inquisitors with good humour, offering a nod and a half-smile.

In the next room along, Margaret Pepys lay still in her four-poster bed, covered by a heavy woollen blanket; a white cat lay curled up asleep near her feet. So still was

Margaret that the three of them stopped in the doorway and held their breath, until the faint rise of her chest signalled she was still alive, and they exhaled in relief.

Suddenly, from downstairs, there came a hammering on the door, followed by Bulstrode Bennett's bellowing voice: "Open this door at once! I hold in my hand a Letter of Marque signed by Sir Edward Mallory himself! Jacob Standish, Abigail Harcourt, show yourselves! You were witnessed entering this dwelling!"

His ranting woke even the ailing Mistress Pepys.

## Chapter Twenty-Two

# Figures in Shadow

When Abby woke the following morning, she found herself on a cold stone floor and in total darkness. It took her a while to figure out where she was and how she came to be there. The dawning realisation made her cry out angrily. *Bettered by Bulstrode Bennett*, she thought. *Such are men and their power.*

Jacob woke around the same time, though it was impossible to tell whether it was day or night, as his cell also had no windows. The previous night, he and Abby had been marched, their hands bound, to a square stone lock-up opposite the church, and thrown in separate cells. They had been stripped of their clothing and few possessions by a Brampton constable, and made to wear filthy prison rags.

Bennett had discovered Abby's list of suspects. Upon seeing his own name, he tore the parchment to shreds before her eyes.

"How dare you think that I would stoop so low as to be involved in the killing of Goddie Grimston," he told her. "The pathetic wretch met his end at the hands of your witches, as everyone well knows. Simon Hopkins will prove that. And I hear that the witch-finder draws near."

"Is anybody there?"

Abby and Jacob both heard it. They recognised the voice as well.

"Rebecca?" they called back in unison.

"Silence in there!" came the faint male voice, from outside the jail.

A key turned in a lock, and a heavy door creaked open. Muted daylight entered the three prisoners' cells through the small barred window in their doors, and each averted their eyes.

"You shall not speak," ordered the local constable, John Ward, who had been stationed outside by the magistrate. (The prisoners might have raised a smile, had they known the weather had turned for the worse overnight and his clothing was wet through.)

"May I light a candle, pray?" Abby asked.

They all caught the constable's impatient sigh.

Shortly, each of them was chewing on stale bread, while a weak, flickering flame illuminated their grim surroundings. The cells were so small that Jacob had had to sleep with his head propped awkwardly against one wall and his feet jammed against the one opposite. The walls were slimy and smelled of mildew. From the stonework, Abby suspected the lock-up was part of the ecclesiastical complex connected to the church of St Mary Magdalen.

On the positive side, the inquisitors had prepared for this; a messenger was already heading to London on horseback. But how long would it be before Mr Pepys's reply came, while they endured these atrocious conditions?

Which still left the unfortunate Rebecca Thacker, accused of witchcraft now thrice: concerning Goddie's spoiled crops; concerning his death; and now lately the sickness of John and Margaret Pepys. With Hopkins riding to Brampton, the omens looked ill.

After John Ward returned to his post outside, they found they were able to communicate in whispers, faces pressed against the bars in their doors, without alerting him.

Abby could not see Jacob in the adjacent cell, but she could see Rebecca in the one opposite.

The clothier's face looked haggard, its furrows enhanced in the shadows of her candlelight. "What am I to do?" she implored the inquisitors. "You were supposed to be our salvation, yet Bennett now has you confined beside me."

When Jacob explained their ruse involving Samuel Pepys and the messenger, he expected it would quell her fears.

Instead, she began to weep and tugged uselessly on her iron bars. "Then you'll be free while I rot in this cell!" She sank to the floor, her face vanishing from view.

There was no option but to let her tears run dry.

At length, she recovered her composure. "I've always prided myself on being strong and independent," Rebecca said, sniffling. "But these charges have brought me to my knees. I truly fear the next time I see the flowers I so love, a noose will be waiting for me."

"Tell us about yourself," said Abby.

Rebecca screwed up her eyes quizzically.

"Tell us about yourself," Abby repeated. It would help take her mind off the dire situation, she hoped.

Rebecca Thacker was born in Brampton in 1640, in the house where she still resided, she explained. Her parents, Eliza and Matthew, were both weavers, and she grew up enchanted by their craft.

Her mother would take her out into the meadows and hedgerows, pointing out the different wildflowers that could be used in the alchemy of dye-crafting. It became her passion, and she wandered far from home, seeking out fresh glades and hollows where different species might lurk.

Their family had been torn apart when Matthew joined Cromwell's New Model Army. Rebecca was just nine, she recalled, when her mother told her he had been killed at the Battle of Maidstone.

Afterwards, she became apprenticed under her mother's wing and found herself making clothing to sell at market, at which she appeared to have a natural talent. Her mother never fully recovered from the death of her husband, Rebecca said, which weakened her spirit and brought down her so low that she could no longer work.

Eventually, when she was 14, Rebecca's aunt came and took her mother away. Mother and daughter never saw one another again, and she was left to run the family business alone. It was a role in which she thrived. "I had no time, nor need, for a husband," she said.

Specialising in creating colours unseen before, her talent became celebrated throughout the local counties. "But 'tis through my work with herb and potion that I'm accused of witchcraft," Rebecca concluded bitterly.

Jacob, who had listened intently to her tale, felt an increased desperation to help the wronged woman. "Is there nought you can tell us, dear lady, that might aid our investigation?"

Rebecca pondered for a while and seemed caught in two minds.

"Pray tell," Jacob urged her.

"There is something… Last week, I delivered garments to his lordship at the manor late one night. I saw, under the moonlight, two figures enter the gardener's cottage on the estate."

"Is that unusual?" asked Abby.

"I believe it was. The gardener, who tended the gardens for as long as anybody can remember, died last spring and is yet to be replaced. His cottage should have been empty."

"Did you recognise the figures?" asked Jacob.

Rebecca slowly shook her head, mentally reliving the scene. "I did not. It was too dark. But it appeared to be a man and a woman."

Jacob pursed his lips. "A couple cloaked in shadows conducting a secret affair? How would that relate to Grimston's death and witchery?"

"This small English village, so peaceful and benign to the casual observer, seethes beneath the surface with secrets and lies, Jacob," Abby replied. "If these people have something to hide, we must discover what that is."

Chapter Twenty-Three

---

# The Visitor

The three prisoners eventually grew tired of whispering and each settled into a corner of their cell, passing the time as best they could. Abby mulled over the facts of the case, hoping to alight on something she had missed. Jacob found a stone and tossed it up, trying to catch it in the dim light. Eventually it landed on his candle, knocking it over and extinguishing the flame, thus ending the game.

At some point, Constable Ward re-entered the lock-up bearing sustenance, such as it was. They assumed the hour to be early afternoon, since it coincided with their second meal of the day, traditionally a hearty dinner; in this case, more stale bread and weak ale. Still they consumed it greedily.

Abby grew to wondering who the figures were that Rebecca had seen entering the abandoned gardener's cottage. Were they villagers already under scrutiny by herself and Jacob, or others as yet unknown to them?

Were new suspects about to enter their investigation? She groaned to herself at the thought; this case was troubling enough as it was.

If, as she hoped, these two people did indeed have connections to their case, then what were those connections? While she had pieced together a few theories, there was nothing yet solid enough to share with her fellow inquisitor.

*If only I were free!* she thought to herself. *I could visit the gardener's cottage on the estate and search for clues.*

Bulstrode Bennett had much to answer for.


Several dreary and uncomfortable hours later – presumably supper time, Jacob hoped – the constable's key turned again in its lock and the door creaked open. He had never been so hungry in his life. Oddly, despite the terrible conditions, his cough had eased and his chest felt lighter. He was beginning to think that jail may not be as unhealthy as people made it out to be, until he realised how ridiculous that sounded.

Hunched and morose, Abby was whisked from her introspection. She could hear two male voices, she realised, and neither of them was Jacob's. One was Ward's, but the other…

A face appeared at her barred window, illuminated from below by a hand-held oil lamp, outlined by long raven-black hair and a beard, topped with a broad-brimmed hat. The eyes were lost in shadows. In the visitor's gloved hand was a long wooden staff, and he wore a cape.

A sneer crossed his cold lips.

She knew who he was.

Simon Hopkins had arrived.

"The servant of the witches!" he declared theatrically. "God will judge you also, mark my words, Abigail Harcourt. You shall not escape his earthly vengeance."

How would she react? Abby had wondered this from the moment she knew of Hopkins's involvement in the witchcraft at Brampton. This was the son of the man who had effectively signed her father, the kind and progressive Ambrose Harcourt's, death warrant.

She had read Matthew Hopkins's book and remembered the engraving in its frontispiece. Simon, standing before her now, was dressed in his father's image. She knew where she stood. But… it troubled her: could a son be blamed for his father's actions?

Abby pushed herself to her feet. She would not be overawed by this man, since that is what he wanted. Equally, she knew, she would be wise not to antagonise him. The battle of wits would be won only over time.

"I've been looking forward to making your acquaintance, *Simon Hopkins*." She spoke his name loudly, to alert the others.

It worked. She heard shuffling in the other cells, and Rebecca appeared at her window, riven with awe and fear.

Jacob's voice came: "You have no authority to practice your charlatan trade here, Simon Hopkins."

The witch-finder's head turned to face him, smiling arrogantly. "*Charlatan trade!* I applaud thee, Jacob Standish. However, I have in my possession a Commission for the Discovery of Witchcraft in Brampton, signed by the magistrate himself, Bulstrode Bennett. Pray, where is thy commission?" He paused, his voice dripping with mockery. "Mr Standish?"

*The title of Hopkins's Commission, so close to that of his father's infamous* Discovery of Witches, thought Abby. It was no coincidence.

Jacob, meanwhile, was babbling. "'Tis true that… That we do not possess…"

Hopkins pressed a gloved finger to his lips. "Hush, Mr Standish. I will speak with the witch now."

The witch-finder turned towards Rebecca, who began whimpering. His eyes widened with menace, freezing her in terror.

"Speak, witch!" Hopkins commanded.

She could not.

Abby was no longer able to hold her tongue. "Can't you see that she's terrified?" she called out. "Rebecca Thacker is no witch, you monster!"

"The Lord God Almighty shall be her judge!" Hopkins exclaimed. Then he twisted suddenly, his features contorted with rage. Pointing his staff at her, he roared, "Not you, Abigail Harcourt!"

She fell backwards, such was the force of his words, and lay sprawled on the hard, wet, gritty floor.

"Bring the witch, Mr Ward," she heard him order, and a key turning in Rebecca's door.

"She shall join her fellow sorceress, Paulina Pepys," said Hopkins. "And soon we shall hear their confession."

Abby scrambled to her feet and pressed her face against the bars. "You have Paulina?"

The witch-finder smiled.

The door closed, plunging her back into darkness.

# Chapter Twenty-Four

---

# A Seal Broken

The inquisitors spent another miserable day in the damp, stale air. Their minds were fraught with images of Paulina and Rebecca quailing at the mercy of Simon Hopkins, and they cursed their inability to act.

Jacob noticed his persistent cough had completely ceased. He felt better than he had done in several days, although his stomach rumbled terribly, echoing around his tiny cell, which only made his hunger worse.

Abby barely slept, chilled to the marrow, consumed by guilt and anger. Anger at herself for being outwitted by Bennett and Hopkins, but more, far more, she was angry at those two men. Men who abused their power in the name of God and the greater good.

Around late afternoon, a heated exchange reached Abby's ears from outside the lock-up. The next thing she knew, a key was turning in the lock on Jacob's door. Constable Ward's face appeared at her window, then disappeared as he bent down to unlock her door.

In a daze, she forced her aching limbs to work and half-stumbled out of her cell. The main door was open, and she inhaled deeply, savouring the fresh air.

A man was standing with Ward, dressed in sturdy leather and wearing a waxed cape. In his hand, he held a furled sheet of parchment and a wax-sealed letter that he handed to Jacob. "I came as soon as I could, sir," he said.

The letter was addressed to: Mr Jacob Standish, The Bull Inn, Brampton.

Jacob broke the wax seal and read aloud.

"Sir, As you did request, I have dispatched with your messenger the Special Commission of Enquiry, duly signed by the Lord High Admiral of England, James Stuart, Duke of York. It does authorise your continued investigations throughout Huntingdonshire, and woe betide any man who stands in your way.

I am much troubled by the gravity of your situation. Unfortunately, I am presently engaged in Navy business of the utmost urgency. The moment my duties are concluded, I shall make haste to Brampton. I will endeavour to arrive before the witch-finder Hopkins. Until that time, the safety of my sister, Paulina, rests in your hands. I pray you repay my trust in you.

Yours sincerely,

Samuel Pepys

Clerk of the Acts."

Jacob looked at Abby. Her grey woollen prison attire
was matted and saggy, her face pallid and drained, and
her hands were filthy – but her turquoise eyes, he saw,
blazed with fervour.

"Where is Hopkins?" she demanded of Constable
Ward.

The jailer looked all out of pomp. "I… I heard he has
the women held in the village hall," he stammered.

Despite being cold, wet, hungry and tired, the inquisitors thought only of Paulina and Rebecca. They knew
where the village hall was, having passed it on the way to
the Bennetts's house.

As they walked free into the crisp Brampton afternoon,
the Church of St Mary Magdalen rose silhouetted above
them. Jacob offered up a quick prayer for their success.
To Abby, it was a sign, that theirs alone was the path of
righteousness.

When Jacob tried the door to the village hall, he found
it locked. He shook the handle and barged the heavy,
studded oak, to no avail.

"We'll not gain entry by brute force, Jacob," Abby said,
heading towards the side of the building.

Cupping her hands against a leaded window pane,
shielding her eyes from the light, she peered into the hall

and stiffened. Urgently, she beckoned Jacob. "Look!" she said.

Inside, he made out Paulina Pepys and Rebecca Thacker, seated opposite one another in the middle of the hall. The witch-finder was standing between them, banging his staff into the floor repeatedly, haranguing the women. Paulina's head was bowed, and her shoulders were shaking uncontrollably. Rebecca's red-rimmed eyes stared blankly ahead, transfixed by unseen demons.

Jacob banged on the window and shouted, "Release them immediately!"

The inquisitors saw him drop his staff in shock on seeing them, then hasten towards the front door. They rushed around the building to accost him.

Hopkins was locking the door behind him when they reached him.

"How did you escape?" he demanded. "I shall call for the magistrate."

Jacob handed him their Commission.

Hopkins scanned it, rolled it up and handed it back. "Thou hast friends in high places," he said, arching an eyebrow.

The victory felt good, although it proved to be short-lived.

"Then you will show me your proof that these women are not witches?" Hopkins added, interweaving his gloved fingers.

When neither inquisitor replied, he produced from inside his coat a straw doll, and held it up before them, its lavender scent wafting in the breeze. "Wouldst thou explain this?" he asked innocently.

"'Tis a poppet, as well you know," Abby replied, "discovered at the door of Goddie Grimston's house."

Hopkins shook his head, smiling. "Nay, Abigail Harcourt. Grimston's poppet had a pin in its heart. This one was pierced in the head."

Jacob looked incredulously at Abby, who tried to remain calm despite her pounding temples.

Hopkins was revelling in their discomfort. "You were not aware, am I to believe, that a second victim of the witches was discovered last night in Brampton?"

"You know we were not, Mr Hopkins," Abby replied. "Who is this victim?" Her hands were shaking, and she willed them still.

"His name was Owen Turner, God rest his soul. Thou knowest of him?"

Their blank expressions told Hopkins all he needed.

An unknown character had indeed entered the investigation.

Jacob recovered enough to speak. "How did this fellow Turner die?"

"Of the witches' curse, Mr Standish," Hopkins replied, as if that were the only possible answer. "It provided for me ample reason to apprehend the witch Pepys."

Abby spoke up, "Was Rebecca incarcerated with us at the time of his death?"

"The time of Mr Turner's death is uncertain. His body was cold when the Devil-doll was discovered at his door." Hopkins fell to his knees, his hands raised in fervent prayer. "Lord, grant me the wisdom to cleanse your lands of these foul demons, so they may receive their punishment. I beseech thee, protect me on this path, for it fills me with fear, though I shall not deviate from it."

# Chapter Twenty-Five

# **By Starlight**

Night had fallen by the time Abby and Jacob reached the Pepyses' home. An owl hooted from far across the fields, and the clear sky revealed a tapestry of glinting stars.

Although they were both desperate to investigate the gardener's cottage on the Ravenscourt estate, more pressing was their need to rest and recuperate after their ordeal in jail. Not to do so would be counter-productive, they agreed – and they needed their wits about them.

Additionally, as Jacob pointed out, "Tomorrow is the Sabbath. Hopkins, a devout Puritan, will be compelled to rest and pray."

It gave them a full day to act while he could not.

Since Paulina's parents lived so close to the inn, the inquisitors decided to check on them since their incarcerated daughter could not. Jacob wondered if they were acting out of kindness or guilt for failing to clear her name.

The Pepyses' door was unlocked, so they let themselves in and were surprised to find Paulina's parents feasting on roast beef and vegetables.

John Pepys rose with a concerned expression. "What news of our dear Paulina?" he asked.

"We heard the witch-finder has arrived," Margaret added, pushing away her half-eaten supper. "Where is Paulina?"

Jacob eyed her remaining dinner. "You are fully recovered?" he asked, his tone almost one of disbelief.

Colour had returned to the couple's cheeks; their eyes were brighter and their voices were clearer. There was life in their bones.

The inquisitors explained Paulina's situation and the reason they appeared so bedraggled, softening certain awkward details. John stood behind his wife and hugged her as they listened.

"Can you help clear her of these false charges?" he asked.

"We are your son's personal inquisitors, sir," Jacob replied. "We shall not fail." He hoped he had masked his waning confidence.

"Aye," Abby agreed, hoping the same.

Jacob was astonished by John and Margaret's recovery. Not long ago, they had both seemed near to death.

"I consider it a miracle, Mr Standish," John told him, raising his eyes towards Heaven.

"Are you hungry?" asked Margaret.

Jacob had thought she would never ask.

As Mrs Pepys retired to her kitchen, a thought occurred to Abby. "Mr Pepys," she said. "Are you familiar with Owen Turner?"

"I am. Why do you ask?"

Not wishing to concern him any more than necessary, she replied, "No great matter, his name was mentioned to us."

"He is a legal clerk who works in Huntingdon, but lives here in the village. A loudmouth young fellow with a reputation for drunkenness." John explained. "You may see him staggering to his office each morning."

*Not now, you will not,* thought Jacob.


When Margaret returned with the inquisitors' dinner, John explained how he had started to feel better the morning after they took to their beds. The pain in his chest, the coughing fits, the cold clamminess of his hands and feet - all had dissipated until he felt well enough to rise. To his great surprise, when he checked on Margaret, she was also out of bed and noticeably improved.

When Jacob mentioned he had also been unwell recently, with symptoms remarkably similar to theirs, he did not notice Abby's eyes light up.

# Chapter Twenty-Six

---

# A New Threat

Abby was up before dawn, pounding on Jacob's door. "Jacob, wake up, we have much to do!" She felt rested, and her voice was ebullient.

Both changed into fresh clothing. Jacob's original outfit, the one he had travelled in from London, had been laundered and pressed by the innkeeper's wife. It felt wonderful on his skin after the sodden harshness of his prison attire.

The previous night, on their way back to The Bull from the Pepys's, they had stopped at Rebecca Thacker's house at Abby's behest. Jacob waited obediently while she went inside. When she emerged, he noticed that her satchel looked heavier. When he asked her about it, she remained tight-lipped. She had a hunch, she told him, nothing more; she would need corroboration before raising his hopes.

The inquisitors breakfasted on local sausages with bread and honey. Jacob had cleaned his plate even before Hatty Nettlewood returned to her kitchen. Abby could not finish her last sausage and looked around for the inn's dog, Rusty, who would always finish her scraps. When she could not see him, she called for Hatty.

The innkeeper's wife bustled towards them. "Abby, Abby, I'm at my wits' end," she declared. "That naughty dog ain't been seen in five days now. 'T'ain't like him. He's gone off before, but never so long."

Jacob waited impatiently outside The Bull while Abby returned to her room. When she joined him, he noticed she was carrying a rectangular item wrapped in cloth, which appeared to be a book. He enquired about it.

"Time is short, Jacob," she replied, ignoring his query. "We head to Ravenscourt Manor, where we'll each take different paths. I, on an errand, while you seek out the gardener's cottage and hunt for clues to the identity of Rebecca's mysterious figures."

Jacob adjusted his periwig. "Will you not assist me?" he asked.

"I have full faith in you," she replied, squeezing his arm. "You are proving to be a fine inquisitor, just as my master knew you would be. Your eye for a clue surpasses mine. If there's one to be found, I fully trust you will find it. Have faith in yourself."

Jacob looked unconvinced. "I would be happier if…"

"Come," she said, heading towards the manor house.

He stood there for a while, watching her steadfast form recede. If only I had half her wits, he thought to himself.

In a daze of admiration, he shook his head and loped after her.

On passing through the estate gatehouse, the inquisitors could make out the lugubrious features of the servant, Edgar, glaring at them through a vast stained-glass window. Jacob suggested they bypass the main door, "We are known here, and our business is authorised." Abby readily agreed.

Passing the ornamental gardens, they reached the rear wing of the house where Archibald Bramwell resided. According to Rebecca, the gardener's cottage would be found nestled among young oak trees, facing the physician's wing.

And so it proved. The cottage was a single-storey dwelling with a steeply pitched, thatched roof, its windows shuttered, some 200 yards up a gravel pathway bisecting a lawn. They realised they had noticed it on their previous visit, unaware then of its significance.

It was time, Abby told Jacob, to part company. "Let's meet back at The Bull, in an hour or two."

Jacob was about to point out that neither of them owned a pocket watch when Alice Wilkins appeared, running towards them, shouting unintelligibly.

When she reached them, the stablemaid glowered as she held out a poppet for them to see. It was similar in design to the others and smelled also of lavender, except this one had wispy long hair made from dried grass and had red thread tied around its throat. A female doll, hanged by the neck.

"What is this?" she demanded, shaking it angrily.

"'Tis a poppet," said Abby, having recovered her composure. "One was…"

"I know what it is!" Alice exclaimed. "Who would dare send me such a thing?"

"Where did you find it?" Abby asked.

"It was on my doorstep. I discovered it when I awoke. Foul thing." Angrily, she tossed it into a nearby hedge and stormed off, leaving the inquisitors staring agog at one another.

"The murderer has a fresh victim in his sights," said Jacob, scratching his temple.

"Indeed. But why target the stablemaid?"

When her question was met with puzzled silence, she added, "We must work quickly to resolve the matter. Off to the gardener's cottage with you, Jacob. And be quick – time is of the essence."

She watched him stride down the path and try the cottage door. When it opened and he disappeared inside, she glanced in his direction before setting off in the opposite direction.

# Chapter Twenty-Seven

# The Cottage

Jacob had expected the interior of the gardener's cottage to smell musty and for its furnishings to be covered in a layer of dust, given that the previous occupant had passed away some time ago. As soon as he entered, he saw that was not the case.

Opening the shutters to allow more light in, he surveyed the scene. A single wooden bed was in the middle of the room, opposite a stone-cold fireplace. The pillows were silk, and the bed was covered in plush red velvet. Hardly the bedding of an aged gardener, Jacob thought to himself.

The kitchen area at the far end looked spotless and unused. The whitewashed walls were bare, except for a fine floral tapestry hanging to the right of the bed. Beside it was a scroll-legged table with a looking glass. The area to the left of the bed was plain and sparse, with only a wooden chest against the wall.

What was this scene telling him? *Think, Jacob!* he urged himself. *You're an inquisitor now. This is your realm.*

It struck him: one side was occupied by a man, the other by a woman. Rebecca's shadowy figures... *They were indeed a couple.*

There was a small, shallow drawer on the underside of the lady's table, which he opened. Inside was a bottle of perfume, which looked to be full. When he opened it and sniffed, the scent was distinctive: sandalwood and mint.

Jacob moved around the bed to investigate the chest. Although it felt disappointingly empty as he lifted the lid, when he peered inside, he found a single, folded white silk handkerchief. Opening out the handkerchief, feeling the softness against his outstretched palm, he saw in one corner an embroidered initial: B.

*Bulstrode Bennett!* It had to be; the initial and the perfume – Bennett's favourite – were unmistakable. *So Bennett was engaged in an illicit affair?* He could imagine as much of the arrogant fellow.

*But,* he wondered, *with whom?*

Two women they knew of in the village wore the sandalwood-and-mint perfume. One was Helen Bennett – who was married to Bulstrode, albeit unhappily – the other was... Alice Wilkins.

*Wilkins and Bennett? Could it really be?* It would explain her silver chain and silk handkerchief – gifts, surely, since a stablemaid could never afford such luxuries.

There was only one way to find out: confront the woman. He hardly needed Abby Harcourt's assistance for that! He would investigate and solve the matter himself, as he had dreamed of doing. Of course, he would give ample plaudits to his fellow inquisitor, who had chipped in here or there.

Jacob's daydream shattered as he neared the Ravenscourt stable block and spotted a female figure on horseback, racing towards Huntingdon. The rider, he could make out, was Alice Wilkins.

# Chapter Twenty-Eight

# To Battle

J acob entered The Bull to find Abby already seated, and she leapt up when she saw him.

"What did you discover?" she asked eagerly. "Pray, be seated. Tell me everything, Jacob, and be quick. We have urgent business elsewhere."

Barty Nettlewood poured a half-pint of beer for Jacob and set down bread and cheese. When he went to replenish Abby's tankard, she held a hand over it, shaking her head. To Jacob's horror, she also sent the food back.

"Sup quickly, Jacob," she told him.

Still, there was no sign of Rusty the dog.

When Jacob laid out his findings - Bennett and the stablemaid involved in an affair, citing her silver and silk - Abby was neither as enthused nor as impressed as he had hoped.

"We should be wary of leaping to conclusions," she told him.

"But... The embroidered letter B?"

"It could be Bramwell," she said, then motioned toward the innkeeper. "Or Barty Nettlewood. What if our couple is not Bulstrode and Alice, but Bramwell and Helen? Or Barty and Alice? Or Barty and…"

Jacob held his hand up for her to stop, and bowed his head.

Abby placed her hand on the back of his. "Nay, you are right, Jacob. The most likely suspect is indeed the magistrate, who was at such pains to thwart our investigation. If that's the case then we must ask ourselves: how does this affair connect with the Brampton witch murders? Come!"

She was up and out of the door before he could protest. Downing the remainder of his beer in one, he waved to Barty and followed.

The innkeeper just managed to call out, "You haven't paid for…," as the door swung shut.

For once, Jacob struggled to keep up with Abby, who was running faster than he had ever seen, racing past the church towards the T-junction. "Where are we heading?" he called out, but received no reply.

He caught up with her as she stopped at the path to the Bennetts's front door, gathering breath.

"Why… are we here?" Jacob asked, also gasping after the exertion.

Abby banged on the door. "Simon Hopkins is here as a guest of the magistrate."

The servant, Benjamin, answered. Before he could utter a word, Bulstrode Bennett appeared and shooed him away. His attire was no less garish than before – the requisite ribbons and pearls hung there – however today the colour scheme was crimson with silver detailing.

The gaunt man regarded the inquisitors with disgust. "When will you return to London?" he snapped. "You have had warning enough."

With Jacob looming menacingly behind her, Abby refused to be intimidated. "We seek an audience with Mr Hopkins," she told the magistrate firmly.

"I fear you have been misinformed. Mr Hopkins is not here," Bennett replied. "He is interrogating the witches in the village hall."

Jacob blurted out, "But today is the Sabbath!"

Bennett smiled smugly. "The witch-finder has made peace with his God. I suggest you take issue with he, not I."

The door slammed shut.

"He labours on a Sunday!" exclaimed Jacob.

Abby bit her lip. "He's outfoxed us, Jacob. We haven't a moment to lose."

They had passed the village hall only minutes ago and could see it set among trees from where they stood, wreathed in shadows.

"How dare thee question my faith!" the witch-finder thundered, when Jacob questioned his decision to work on the Sabbath. "My quest is the Lord's quest: to root out evil wherever it doth fester. Thus do I honour him even on this sacred day."

Hopkins was becoming desperate, which only made him more dangerous.

Paulina and Rebecca sat where they had before, looking even more forlorn, frightened and defeated. Pepys's sister did not even look up when they entered the hall; Rebecca managed the briefest of pitiful glances. It was apparent that neither woman had slept.

They had been joined by two other women, both strangers to the inquisitors. These women were not being interrogated, that was obvious; they were too fresh-faced, and their clothing looked relatively fresh. One was in her late-teens, the other in her mid-thirties. The younger woman stared at the ground. Both wore peasant garb of linen dress with apron, and white cotton cap.

Hopkins spoke. "Are you acquainted with Dorothy and Eleanor Brooks?"

When Abby and Jacob shook their heads, he continued, "Mother and daughter. They are…"

The younger of the two shot Abby a guilty look.

"They are your watchers, Mr Hopkins," Abby interjected. "Your work here is tantamount to torture, sir."

The witch-finder laid a gloved hand on Paulina's shoulder, and she flinched.

"My work here is the Lord's work, Abigail," he retorted calmly. "You shall find nought untoward. Magistrate Bennett will support me in this."

It was time for Abby to play her hand.

Reaching into her bag, she pulled out a folded sheet of parchment and held it out for Hopkins to take. He stood still, suspicious, stroking his beard.

"Take it, Mr Hopkins," she said. "It's a Declaration, signed by Lord Fairfax's physician, Archibald Bramwell."

Eyeing her warily, the witch-finder took the parchment and unfolded it.

"It states that John and Margaret Pepys were not the victims of a witch's curse…," Abby began.

Rebecca managed to raise her head, her sleep-deprived eyes intent upon Abby.

"…but that they were the unwitting victims of poisoning by lead."

Hopkins bellowed with mocking laughter. Abby simply talked over him, explaining the deductions of the letter aloud.

The key to her deduction, she explained, was Jacob's illness. His symptoms - cold hands, cough, shortness of breath, among others - were the same as John and Margaret Pepys's. It had made Abby wonder: *What do they and Jacob have in common? Did they eat the same food, or inhabit the same foul space?*

Then it had struck her: they wore the same yellow undergarments, made by the same clothier, using the same dye. "What if that dye contained a harmful substance?" Abby asked, "which might cause illness, unbeknown to the woman who concocted it: Rebecca Thacker?"

Hopkins's laughter ceased. Abby now had everybody's full attention.

"That yellow pigment, I purchase from an apothecary in Cambridge," Rebecca told her. "Then mix it with others of my own devising. It is no poison."

"You can't be certain of that," Abby replied. "Neither could I, knowing nought of the composition of dyes. Then I remembered the book we had been given, on our journey here."

Jacob slapped his thigh. "The book on dyes by Humphrey Worthington!"

Hopkins snorted dismissively.

"The book on dyes by Humphrey Worthington," Abby repeated, beginning to relish her role of inquisitor. "*Of Dyes and Dyeing: A Detailed Compendium of the Art and Science of Colouring Fabrics*, and so on, to relate but part of its title."

Worthington's text gave credence to her theory, she explained. However, she knew she would need a physician - ideally one who experimented with poisons - to confirm it. Thus, with Jacob employed elsewhere, she had visited Archibald Bramwell.

Abby explained that she had taken the specific yellow dye to him, having found a jar of it at Rebecca's cottage the night before. Bramwell tested it and confirmed that it contained lead, which he explained could poison a man given sustained contact. The Pepyses routinely wore their yellow undergarments, and Jacob had even slept in his shirt, which clung to his skin - this confirmed Abby's theory.

"Indeed," she concluded, pointing at the letter in the witch-finder's hand, "Bramwell signed his name to it."

Hopkins glared down at the physician's Declaration, his brow tightly furrowed, quietly simmering. Rebecca keenly studied his expression; Paulina still had not moved.

"What of the curse on Grimston's crops?" Hopkins said at last. "Or the death of Grimston himself? Thou doth not disprove sorcery at work in these instances."

Jacob spoke up, aware that the situation called for his authority. "Abigail Harcourt has cast doubt upon your case against the clothier, Rebecca Thacker. Lord Fairfax's physician himself states that John and Margaret Pepys were poisoned by lead, not laid low by witchcraft as you assert. It would not reflect well in any trial of the woman."

Hopkins smirked. "Doest thou forget Bulstrode Bennett, Mr Standish?"

"Do you forget the Senior Magistrate, Sir Edward Mallory, Mr Hopkins?" he retorted.

Bulstrode had warned Hopkins about Mallory: the Senior Magistrate preferred a quiet life free from controversy, and would leave them alone as long as Hopkins's investigation ran smoothly. Hopkins knew he dare not trigger Mallory's involvement.

The witch-finder slammed his staff into the floor in anger. "Very well!" he roared. "I shall free the clothier…"

Rebecca gasped, burying her head in her hands as sobs wracked her body. Even Paulina managed to twist her head towards her friend, though she did not have the energy to raise a smile.

But Hopkins had not finished. "…However, the witch Pepys doth remain here. For tonight she shall summon her imps."

# Chapter Twenty-Nine

# A Few Ales

The inquisitors were back at The Bull. They found themselves embracing its gentle homeliness, so far removed from the ruckus and ribaldry of a London inn. They had grown fond of the eccentric innkeeper and his wife. The food was good, too. They had both noticed how ready access to such fresh rural produce offered noticeable improvements in flavour.

It being a Sunday, the inn's door was customarily closed. Since they were guests, and the innkeeper was no slave to piety, they had been served ale with their supper. When Jacob called for more, Barty Nettlewood locked the front door and obliged him.

It had been an encouraging day, with one of the so-called Brampton witches now free. As heady and affirming as it was, neither Abby nor Jacob could shake the suspicion that they had freed the wrong woman first. Samuel Pepys had engaged them to save his sister.

If Simon Hopkins saw his prospects of a successful witch-hunt fading, he would become more reckless and so more ruthless in his pursuit - with solely Paulina in his sights. The unfortunate woman already seemed defeated.

"We have bested Simon Hopkins," Jacob assured Abby, in a celebratory mood.

She remained circumspect. "We shouldn't underestimate him, Jacob. Now that Rebecca's escaped his clutches, he'll act like a baited bear. 'Tis a grave concern."

"Then we must clear Paulina's name!" Jacob declared.

"That's what we have endeavoured to do since we arrived in Brampton," she pointed out. "And I wonder, are we any closer to doing so?"

Jacob pushed his grinning face towards hers. "Your performance today! You held Hopkins like an insect and crushed him!"

She backed away from his beery breath. "That is precisely my concern, Jacob. He won't take defeat lightly."

"But Abby, you are an inquisitor! Mr Samuel Pepys's inquisitor! Soon we shall be esteemed throughout the land!"

"No, Mr Standish. I'm a maidservant. Master Pepys's maidservant. And that is all I shall ever be."

Looking confused, he changed his approach. "Then how do we prove that Bennett is the murderer?"

"You assume that he is."

"For certain, he is!"

Jacob detailed the magistrate's suspicious behaviour: having them jailed to stop their investigation; his likely affair with Alice Wilkins; his curious disinterest in what turned out to be Goddie Grimston's death throes…

Abby found herself joining in. "That he was present on the night of Goddie's death makes him a primary suspect. Then there's the deadly nightshade you saw growing beside his stable…"

Lost in the haze of Barty's ale, she was becoming convinced herself.

Chapter Thirty

# The Morning After

Abby awoke to the sound of rain beating on the window. Her head was pounding. *Curse that wicked ale,* she thought to herself, and was surprised to hear Jacob already up and about.

"Woken by an infernal cockerel!" he told her, to her mild amusement.

They skipped breakfast - although both craved sustenance - and headed immediately for the village hall, wordless in their urgency. The rain was heavy, dark clouds hung low, and the livestock huddled together in the fields.

Disconcertingly, they noticed the hall door was wide open as they approached. Inside, they found the witch-finder speaking with his watchers, Dorothy and Eleanor Brooks, both with dark circles under their eyes, looking fit to collapse.

A white cat - Sugar, the Pepyses' cat - lay curled on a windowsill, regarding the proceedings through slitted eyes.

Simon Hopkins spread his arms wide as Abby and Jacob entered. "Mr Samuel Pepys's esteemed inquisitors!" he hailed, his voice laden with sarcasm. "Thy master hath but lately departed."

They exchanged glances. "Mr Pepys was here?" Jacob asked, surprised.

"Indeed. And so greatly troubled," the witch-finder replied, all mock sincerity.

"Why, sir?" Jacob demanded.

"Hast thou not heard? Last night his sister confessed to witchcraft, having summoned forth her foul imp." Hopkins pointed at the cat.

Young Eleanor Brooks dared to speak up. "He fetched it," she said quietly. "She didn't summon it."

The witch-finder raised his hand as if to strike her, and she cowered. "Silence, blasphemer! Would you join the other witch in jail?"

Jacob advanced on Hopkins, who stood his ground. "Paulina Pepys is in jail?"

Hopkins's lips curled into a sneer. "She is a witch, sir, and hath committed murder through her cursed demons. Where else would a witch be? Word hath been sent to

Magistrate Bennett, who will arrive forthwith, and we shall set in motion her trial."

Jacob straightened to his full height. "Paulina Pepys is no witch. We have good reason to believe that Grimston was murdered by the magistrate himself, Bulstrode Bennett."

Hopkins roared with laughter, encouraging his watchers to join in, which they did half-heartedly. Only Abby and Jacob remained grim-faced.

Abby stamped her foot angrily and spoke above the noise. "If you would listen…?"

Jacob gripped her arm. "Where is Mr Pepys?"

In an instant, the laughter stopped and they saw that the witch-finder's attention was focused on the doorway. A young boy stood there, dripping wet from the rain.

"My messenger!" Hopkins announced. "Pray, where is Magistrate Bennett, boy? I didst order thou to fetch him!"

The child held out a straw doll. "They found him dead in his stable this morning, sir. His wife found this doll at their door. Magistrate Bennett is dead, sir."

Once they had recovered their composure, the inquisitors argued that Paulina could not possibly have been responsible for the magistrate's death. After all, she would have been in jail at the time.

The witch-finder, flustered at the loss of a powerful ally, refused to listen. He ranted about demons and imps,

God and Jesus Christ. There was no counter-argument, only common sense, which he would never hear.

"Thou shalt not suffer a witch to live!" Hopkins exclaimed, raising his staff towards Heaven.

The inquisitors had no choice but to return to The Bull, to plan.

There, they discovered Samuel Pepys.

# Chapter Thirty-One

# Near Hysteria

**M**r Pepys was in a sorry state, his finery soaked through by rain and his mood jittery. Abby had never seen her master so out of sorts.

"Where have you been?" he wailed as they entered The Bull.

He had ridden to Brampton overnight on a hired horse, he told them, his tone one of barely contained hysteria. It had taken him an age to wake anyone when he arrived at the inn in the early hours. The inquisitors guiltily recalled their sound, ale-induced slumbers.

Eventually, he had woken Barty Nettlewood, who informed him of Paulina's interrogation by the witch-finder in the village hall. Panicked, he rode straight there. Upon learning that his sister had been taken to jail by the Brampton constable, he confronted Hopkins.

"Though I argued forcefully, it was to no avail," said Pepys.

Hopkins, it seemed, would always place God above the Clerk of the Acts to the Navy Board.

Realising that his only option was to appeal to a higher legal authority, Pepys told them, he then rode to Huntingdon to seek Sir Edward Mallory's counsel. Not wishing to wake him, he had to wait until the Senior Magistrate rose and granted him an audience.

Mallory agreed, after some cajoling, to come to the Brampton village hall that afternoon, where both sides could state their case. However, he warned Pepys that the Brampton magistrate held final authority in the village. Mallory could only intervene if the law were transgressed.

"And here I am," Pepys concluded, wringing his hands. "Desperate for some good news of your investigation."

Jacob spoke up, avoiding his mentor's gaze. "The Brampton magistrate, Bulstrode Bennett, is dead, sir."

Pepys's mouth fell open. "*Dead?* When did this occur?"

"Early this morning." Jacob flushed with embarrassment. "Unfortunately, we did…"

Abby cut in, "Sir, I have a few theories. What we dearly require is…"

Hatty Nettlewood's shriek from outside interrupted her.

The three of them rushed out and found her pointing, horrified, towards a wooden shed. "'E's in there!" she wailed, covering her face with her apron.

"Who's in there, Hatty?" Abby asked, wrapping her arm around the distraught woman.

"Rusty!" she exclaimed. "An' e's dead! Looks like 'e's been there for days!"

Leaving the sobbing Hatty behind, Abby dashed into the shed. This, she hoped, might be the break she had been waiting for…

# Chapter Thirty-Two

# The Unravelling

Word spread quickly around Brampton that a spectacle was taking place in the village hall. The place was packed when the inquisitors and Mr Pepys arrived. Constable Ward was guarding the door, barring late-comers from entry, but he stood aside when he saw Abby and Jacob, knowing too well their key role in the proceedings.

When Pepys followed, Ward eyed the gentleman's expensive yet bedraggled attire. "Pardon me, sir…" Then recognising the regular Brampton visitor, he exclaimed, "Mr Samuel Pepys! 'Tis a pleasure, sir, to…"

Pepys barged past him, in no mood for pleasantries.

The tense chatter in the room created a constant, low rumble in the new arrivals' ears. A semi-circle of mismatched stools occupied the centre of the hall, facing an ornate armchair where Sir Edward Mallory, the Senior Magistrate, sat. Dressed in a fur-lined, royal-blue robe and freshly powdered, long grey periwig, he was eyeing the room, distaste curled upon his grey lips.

In the semi-circle were seated: Archibald Bramwell, watchers Dorothy and Eleanor Brooks, and the accused woman, Paulina Pepys, which left two stools unoccupied. In the middle stood the witch-finder, Simon Hopkins, stern and defiant. As soon as he spotted Abby and Jacob pushing through the crowd, his gaze never left them.

Packed all around this scene were the villagers: a sea of dirty faces, in hats and coifs, bobbing as they craned to see.

Mallory spotted the inquisitors too, and ordered them to take the two spare seats. When he noticed Pepys following, he motioned for him to stand behind them, then continually indicated for him to move further back. Only when Pepys was squeezed like an urchin up a chimney among the foul-smelling crowd, did Sir Edward appear happy.

Pepys scowled, unaccustomed to occupying the periphery. His face softened when he caught his sister's eye. Paulina, having been fed, had recovered some of her spirit and colour, although her ordeal remained etched upon her face.

Jacob scanned the room for familiar faces and spied the stablemaid, Alice Wilkins, standing behind Bramwell. A few rows behind her was Anne Grimston, partially blocked from his view by a man in an unnecessarily tall hat. He could see that she was arguing with the fellow; shortly, she swiped the hat away and flung it over the crowd's heads.

Towards the rear of the spectators, near the main door, Jacob noticed Barty Nettlewood wearing his omnipresent eye-patch, craning his neck to see, and waved to him. When Abby nudged him, he stopped. The innkeeper had not seen him anyway.

Mallory tapped his silver-topped cane three times into the floor, to gain everyone's attention. When that had no effect, Hopkins slammed down his wooden staff and bellowed, "Silence!" Immediately, a hush descended, and all eyes were drawn to the witch-finder.

…Including Mallory's. The Senior Magistrate fixed Hopkins with a stern gaze, and the crowd collectively held its breath.

"Simon Hopkins, I am the Senior Magistrate of Huntingdonshire," Mallory intoned firmly. (Most present noticed he had not addressed Hopkins as Mr, neatly establishing a hierarchy.) "The tragic demise of the Brampton magistrate, Bulstrode Bennett, does not grant you jurisdiction over these matters."

All eyes slid towards his adversary. "With all due respect, Sir Edward," Hopkins replied calmly, "'tis not the law I answer to, but to The Almighty himself, who hath called upon me to root out the wicked and godless. Such is this foul witch before us, sir." Hopkins pointed his staff at Paulina, who bowed her head, hiding herself away. Loud murmurs broke out.

Mallory rose sharply, the scar on his forehead practically throbbing. "You shall answer to the law of this land, Simon Hopkins, and you shall answer to me!"

Hopkins refused to be intimidated. He could feel the spirit of his father flowing through him. "Sir, I would not need to take matters into mine own hands, had men of law the courage to confront evil where it hides. Thus, I fear, do witches thrive."

The Senior Magistrate's cheek twitched with irritation. "If you continue to act as if you have unchecked authority, *Simon Hopkins*, you shall find yourself in a cell, with no one but the Almighty to answer to!" he roared.

The witch-finder merely smiled. "The Lord's judgment is swift, Sir Edward. If thou doth oppose his will, thou shalt answer for it. For his power is far greater than the legal codes of this land."

Several spectators burst into applause.

Jacob caught Abby's eye and shook his head.

Further back, Samuel Pepys was biting his tongue.


This legal to-and-fro continued, Mallory at boiling point, his adversary supernaturally calm. In the end, Sir Edward had no legal option but to allow Hopkins to state his case.

And so the inquiry began.

The witch-finder began by outlining his involvement: the visit from the Brampton magistrate; the witch's curse on Goddie Grimston; and the farmer's subsequently ruined crops. (Both inquisitors noticed he was careful to exclude the name of Rebecca Thacker from his testimony.)

Hopkins went on to recall how Goddie had received a witch's poppet, laid at his doorstep. Later, he stated, the farmer was subjected to a violent seizure - the witch's curse incarnate - which killed him.

The witch-finder placed his hands on Paulina's shoulders. Tears welled in her eyes and began streaming down her cheeks.

He continued, "This witch hath communed with the Devil himself, through her demon imp, Sugar, whom she did summon in mine presence, and in the presence of these two devout and righteous witnesses, Dorothy and Eleanor Brooks."

The overawed women could only nod.

The village hall was filled with angry murmurs as the crowd swayed and jostled, some at the rear trying to break through to get to Paulina.

Amid the uproar, Abby Harcourt stood.

Hopkins smirked at her, shaking his head as if she were a foolish child. Jacob whispered a quick prayer under his breath.

"SILENCE!" came the cry. It was Samuel Pepys himself.

Shocked by his ferocity, the rabble obeyed without question.

Sir Edward spoke. "I am obliged to you, Mr Pepys. However, do, pray, rest assured that I am able to command my own inquiry."

Pepys nodded, chastened.

The Senior Magistrate continued, "Now, Abigail Harcourt, inquisitor to Mr Pepys. Speak your part."

Abby looked around at the wretched and eager faces, wondering how she had come to this point.

With a quick glance at Jacob, she began. "Sir Edward, 'tis my belief, and the belief of my fellow inquisitor, Mr Jacob Standish, that Goddie Grimston was not the victim of a witch's curse."

A gasp rose in the hall. Hopkins muttered something to himself.

"Goddie Grimston was poisoned, sir."

All hell broke loose.

When the commotion finally ceased, she continued, "I have recently examined The Bull inn's dog, Rusty, which went missing the morning after Goddie passed away. The poor creature had hidden behind barrels, where it died, its eyes wide and its mouth foaming. The same fate that befell the farmer. They were both poisoned with belladonna, sir. Deadly nightshade."

A voice called out, "Then who poisoned them?"

"Goddie Grimston's last words were, 'The b...'. Magistrate Bennett, *who was complicit in the crime...*" Abby had to allow another wave of catcalls and outrage to subside. "Magistrate Bennett, who was complicit in the crime, declared that Grimston was trying to say, 'The Brampton witches'. We, my fellow inquisitor and I, believed he was trying to say, 'The beer', which we considered had been poisoned.

"*Sir, we were all wrong.*"

The tension became palpable as the crowd held its communal, fetid breath.

"Who killed him?" yelled someone.

"Aye!" agreed many others. "Who killed him?"

Abby rolled her shoulders. "Goddie Grimston's dying words were not 'The Brampton witches', but *'The bread'*. Barty Nettlewood provides it for every customer, and Goddie and his wife were partaking of it that night. Goddie noticed the bitterness of the poison in his, but sadly too late. After the shock of his death, the uneaten leftovers were discarded, where poor Rusty scavenged them and suffered the same fate."

Simon Hopkins removed his hat and ran his fingers through his black hair. "She endeavours to deny the Lord his vengeance and will burn in the fires of Hell! The evidence of witchcraft is plain for all to see!"

Sir Edward ignored him and leaned forward in his chair. "Pray explain, Abigail Harcourt, who did bake this poisoned bread?"

"We'd smelled her baking that very afternoon," Abby replied, amid utter silence. "She substituted her poisoned bread for Hatty's, on Goddie's plate, when he was distracted. No doubt while he was drunkenly confronting Jacob. She barters her baked goods for beer at The Bull, so it went unnoticed. The murderer, Sir Edward, is…"

"Anne Grimston!" shrieked Helen Bennett, crashing through the door into the hall, causing everyone's heads to turn. She was waving a sheet of parchment in the air. "Anne Grimston, the conniving whore, has conspired with my gullible-fool husband to change his Will. He leaves all his money and land to her!" With a loud gasp, she promptly and ostentatiously fainted.

Goddie's wife was dragged forward to face the Senior Magistrate.

"What say you for yourself, Anne Grimston?" Sir Edward demanded.

Hopkins stepped in front of her and raised his voice. "Thou overstep thine bounds, Sir Edward! Witchcraft is no ordinary crime. Thou hast no authority over God's judgment!"

"If you have evidence, then present it, Hopkins."

The witch-finder raised a gloved hand. "Sir, if thou wouldst allow me…?" Scrabbling through his coat pockets and finding nothing, he began hunting beneath the stools.

Anne Grimston's arms were pinned behind her back, her blonde plait had become unravelled and there were scratches on her face. She spat on the ground and glared at Helen Bennett, who had been carried forward by four men, and was recovering on the floor at Sir Edward's feet. "He loathed you and sought solace in me," she rasped, struggling to get free.

Somehow instantly revived, Helen went for her and was pulled back by locals. "I thank God you killed him, harlot!" she exclaimed. "But you will never have his money. I earned that, living with the pig!"

Before their exchange could escalate, Simon Hopkins appeared between them. Walking in a tight circle, he held aloft a tool recovered from his bag: a witch-pricking needle.

Despite this dramatic display, many in the crowd paid him no heed, forcing him to shout to be heard. "Sir, this is a craven miscarriage of God's justice! Pray allow me this one test for witchcraft, that I might prove the Pepys woman to be a witch once and for all!"

"Your tests are outdated, Hopkins," Sir Edward told him, with obvious relish. "They belong to another age."

People began jeering, and a chant rose: "Prick the witch! Prick the witch!"

Wretched Paulina Pepys had been forgotten amid the histrionics. Still seated while all around her were standing, she looked up to find all eyes – some angry, some pitying – on her. Overwhelmed, she buried her face in her hands, shaking.

When someone pulled her to her feet, her brother rushed forward and tore the assailant's grip from her arm. Paulina and Samuel caught each other's gaze, and she fell into his arms.

However, the Senior Magistrate was swayed by the crowd's mood to allow Hopkins his final, desperate throw of the dice. And so the scene was set.

Paulina stood with her back bared, hands splayed against a wall. The inquisitors found themselves at the front of an expectant throng, beside Mr Pepys and Sir Edward.

Simon Hopkins paced behind Paulina, muttering prayers with his head bowed. To Abby, it was all pure theatre.

Finally, Hopkins faced the crowd. "Witness me as I prick this woman! If she is a witch, she will not bleed!"

Hopkins turned, the wooden handle of the needle wrapped in his gloved hand, and pushed the point slowly, slowly, into Paulina's back. She appeared to register no pain as the full length of the six-inch needle disappeared into her flesh.

When the witch-finder retracted the point, no mark appeared.

Onlookers crowded in closer, and those nearer the back craned their necks to see.

Hopkins repeated the process. Again, no mark.

Whispered, shocked chatter broke out.

Hopkins turned, eyes heavenward, fists clenched, triumphant. "The Lord is on my side! This devil is indeed a witch!"

Jacob leapt forward, wrenching the witch-pricker from Hopkins's grasp before he could react. Holding his hands aloft so all could see, he pushed the needle into his palm, then again, and again, and again. No wound appeared, and no blood seeped out.

"The handle is hollow!" exclaimed the inquisitor. "The needle is held on a spring!"

Jacob demonstrated, pushing the point of the needle with his fingertip. Its shaft could clearly be seen to disappear into the wooden sheath of a hollowed-out handle.

"'Ere, gimme that!" said a sceptical-sounding onlooker, swiping the witch-pricker off Jacob and repeating the trick. "'E's right!" the man called out. "'Tis fake! This so-called witch-finder's no more 'n a swindler!"

Sir Edward summoned Constable Ward, who bound Simon Hopkins by the wrists, though he did not struggle or attempt to escape. Instead, he prayed.

The Senior Magistrate held him by the throat and growled at him face-to-face. "You did attempt to deceive the law of this land with fakery and chicanery, Simon Hopkins. Knowing full well it was at the expense of an innocent woman's life. Mark my words: you will hang for your deception."

# Chapter Thirty-Three

## Post Mortem

The scene at The Bull inn was one of great jubilation. The Pepys family - John and Margaret, Samuel and Paulina - were reunited in joy, toasting the inquisitors, who had saved Paulina's life and their family's reputation.

Abby wondered which one mattered more to Pepys, though she dared not ask.

Celebratory mead and ale flowed, and Hatty Nettlewood prepared a feast of roasted meats served with an array of early-autumn vegetables - carrots, parsnips, pumpkin, beetroot, kale - and, naturally, bread. Jacob tore a chunk from a loaf, raised it to his lips, hesitated, and returned it to the dish.

Once the meal was finished, the six of them sat around The Bull's largest table, stomachs fit to burst, and John Pepys produced a flageolet, that they might enjoy some music.

His son raised a hand for silence. "Before we carouse, I wish to know more of your investigation," he told Abby and Jacob. "Why, pray, did Anne Grimston choose to involve Paulina in her sinister schemings?"

Jacob looked towards Abby, who was seated opposite him.

"She's incarcerated and will likely hang, so we may never know the whole truth," Abby replied. She let that sink in, and the mood around the table deflate. "But I do have a few theories."

Anne Grimston and Bulstrode Bennett had been carrying on an affair, she explained. Rebecca Thacker had seen them entering the gardener's cottage, where Jacob later found Bulstrode's chest and Anne's perfume. The scent had been given to her by the magistrate, it being his favourite. She clearly did not share his taste in perfume, given Jacob found the bottle to be full.

Bulstrode and Helen Bennett loathed one another. Yet Bulstrode was smitten with the alluring Anne, which she played on, encouraging him to change his Will to exclude his hated wife, Helen, in revenge for the years of married misery.

"Remember when we walked to Huntingdon?" Abby asked Jacob. "We bumped into Anne, who gave us only a glimpse of her legal papers. We know the magistrate was in Huntingdon that same day, and I'm certain those papers didn't concern her husband's legacy, as she told us, but Bulstrode's Last Will and Testament. I'd wager the witness to the signing of those papers was a legal clerk named Owen Turner, whose loud mouth signed his death warrant.

"Anne Grimston was far cleverer and more ruthless than she presented to us."

Samuel tapped the table impatiently. "You ignored my question. Why did this evil woman involve my sister?"

"Because she needed Goddie dead, and what better ploy than witchcraft? Especially if you can browbeat your husband - the murder victim - into making the accusation. 'Tis my guess Anne wanted only Rebecca involved, knowing of your family's reputation, but Goddie's mouth ran away with him. After all, it was Anne herself who had protested Paulina's innocence."

Jacob, who was taking this all in with mounting awe, spoke. "Yet she did murder her lover, the magistrate?"

Abby nodded. "Bulstrode Bennett was wasting away. His wife would confirm it, but I suspect he suffered from consumption. Anne Grimston was content to bide her time till he died, when the changed Will would be revealed. When Rebecca was proven innocent of witchcraft, she saw her plan unravelling and panicked. She murdered Bulstrode to hasten the reading of the Will and to increase the suspicion of Paulina's witchery.

"She never loved Bulstrode Bennett. I doubt she loved any man, yet she could wrap them around her finger.

Anne Grimston loved only wealth, which she will never have."

"One final question, pray," said Jacob. "What of Alice Wilkins's chain and handkerchief? If they were not given to her by Bulstrode Bennett, then by whom?"

"Nay, I believe they were given to her by Bennett, Mr Standish," Abby replied. "But not for love. The stablemaid was having an affair with the physician, Bramwell, and they kept it secret from Lord Fairfax. Did you notice she called him 'Archie'? It struck me as overly familiar, and it raised my suspicions."

Jacob could only tip his hat in admiration.

Abby continued, "The physician, who lives opposite the gardener's cottage, knew of Anne and Bulstrode's affair but wisely kept it to himself, aware of the magistrate's influence with Fairfax. He told only his lover, Alice, who then blackmailed Bennett. When Anne found out, she sent Alice a poppet."

Jacob slapped his forehead, "When I looked inside Anne Grimston's house, there was lavender hanging there!" he exclaimed. "Naturally, she had access to straw as the wife of a crop farmer. *It was she who made the poppets.* If only I had realised at the time."

"We probably saved Alice Wilkins's life," Abby concluded.

The Pepys family broke into a spontaneous round of applause. Abby beamed, but noticed that Jacob looked crestfallen.

Samuel patted the big man's arm. "What troubles you, Mr Standish?"

"Sir, I cannot allow myself credit for Abigail's masterful deductions. She is a remarkable inquisitor and I…"

Samuel Pepys stood (slightly wobbly on his feet), to address Jacob formally. "Sir, you alone saved Paulina's life, when you showed Hopkins's witch-pricker to be hollow."

Jacob raised his eyebrows thoughtfully, nodded to himself, and straightened his periwig. "The needle appeared loose, sir. It was but a small matter, sir - a mere trifle."

Abby scuttled around the table and pulled him to his feet.

To John she exclaimed, grinning, "Please, Mr Pepys, play your flageolet! Let us dance!"

---

# Chapter Thirty-Four

# To London

J acob slept in the next morning. A force of habit roused Abby and her master before the sun had risen, though both were suffering from sore heads.

Abby handed Pepys a letter she had written to Sir Edward Mallory, asking that he ensure its safe delivery. It read:

> *To the Honourable Sir Edward Mallory,*
>
> *I write to you regarding Simon Hopkins, the self-appointed witch-finder.*
>
> *Though entrenched in his beliefs to the exclusion of all others, I believe him to be an honourable man. He truly believes his path is righteous and that demons stalk the land. If we do not share those beliefs, it does not make him evil.*
>
> *His only transgression of the law has been the faked witch-pricking tool, which he employed when he was desperate. I respectfully request that you show him leniency, Your Honour.*

*I would wish to extend to Simon Hopkins the humanity that his father denied to mine.*
*Yours faithfully,*
*Abigail Harcourt*

The Nettlewoods saw them off, remarking that they had never before witnessed such excitement in Brampton, and expressed their hopes for a swift return. As a parting gift, Barty gave each of them one of his spare eye-patches, winking cheekily from beneath his own.

Mr Pepys had ordered a stagecoach, which awaited them outside. As the three of them settled in for the journey back to London, Jacob asked him, "Sir, what next for your inquisitors? Will we be retired now that the Brampton witch murders are solved?"

Pepys almost choked. "Good heavens, Mr Standish! Your work as my personal inquisitor has only just begun! I have already in mind a most perplexing case, which may baffle even you…"

# Are you ready for...

Amazon link: mybook.to/pdm-ebook

"I loved this even more than the first one" — *Bookworm Stephanie*

# Ellis Blackwood

Ellis Blackwood fell in love with the writings of Samuel Pepys, and the 17th-century England he so colourfully portrays, via the great man's published diaries. The Samuel Pepys Mysteries are the result of that literary love affair.

Ellis lives on the coast of Cornwall with his wife, two daughters and dog, Spike. A former journalist, he wrote features for many of the UK's most popular national newspapers and magazines. He recently gained an MA in Comedy Writing from Falmouth University.

### The Samuel Pepys Mysteries
Book 1: The Brampton Witch Murders
Book 2: The Plague Doctor Murders
Book 3: The Coffee House Murders
Book 4: The King's Court Murders
Book 5: The Frost Fair Murders

If you've enjoyed this dip into 17th century England – one of the most fascinating periods in England's history – why not join the Pepysaholics? Visit my website to sign up – you'll receive my monthly newsletter, delving into all things Pepys and 17th century, plus the latest Pepys Mysteries news. You'll also receive a **free copy** of the 13,000-word introductory novella, *Mr Pepys's Stolen Diaries*, where we first meet Samuel, Abby and Jacob.

I'm on Facebook and Instagram. Love to hear your thoughts, always happy to answer any questions. Find all my links using this QR code:

# Acknowledgements

I could not have published The Brampton Witch Murders without the sterling work of Tim Brown, whose covers are a joy to behold, and whose editorial guidance has been a godsend. Equally, my wife, Sinead, has worked tirelessly and generously in the background to allow me the time and space to write. Thanks also to Charles Johnston, narrator of The Pepys Mysteries audiobooks, for additional editing of the manuscript.

Researching Samuel Pepys, the period and witchcraft was a great deal of fun. If you'd like to delve into the same, I recommend starting here…

- *The Illustrated Pepys* edited by Robert Latham, Penguin Books (1979)

- *London and the 17th Century* by Margarette Lincoln, Yale University Press (2021)

- *Samuel Pepys: The Unequalled Self* by Claire Tomalin, Penguin Books (2003)

- *Witchfinders* by Malcolm Gaskill, John Murray (2006)

Printed in Great Britain
by Amazon